THE NOVELIZATION

Also by

Lyn Sisson-Talbert and David E. Talbert

The Square Root of Possible

THE NOVELIZATION

Lyn Sisson-Talbert and David E. Talbert

RAZORBILL

An imprint of Penguin Random House LLC, New York

First published in the United States of America by Razorbill,
an imprint of Penguin Random House LLC, 2020

Visit us online at penguinrandomhouse.com.

Library of Congress Cataloging-in-Publication Data is available.

ISBN 9780593203804

Printed in the United States of America

1 3 5 7 9 10 8 6 4 2

Design by Maria Fazio
Text set in Amasis MT Pro

For Elias

Never be afraid when people don't
see what you see. Only be afraid
if you no longer see it.

Love,
Mommy and Daddy

JANGLES AND THINGS

260 Chancer Street, Cobbleton

June 20th, 1890

Dear Jessica,

I wish I could make up for all my faults as a parent. I wanted you to have the world. Reach into the heavens, pull down the stars, just so they could shine on you. Not just read about a happily ever after; I wanted to be the one to give it to you. Jeronicus Jangle, the greatest inventor of all, who only wishes he were the greatest father of all.

With love,

Jeronicus

To anyone who's ever seen the magic

dancing in the flames of their heart.

Once upon a time,

many, many years ago,

stood the most magnificent shop

that ever there was . . .

Jangles and Things.

Chapter One

The shop sat smack-dab on a little lane in the snowy town of Cobbleton.

Despite the ice-capped mountains shielding it on all sides, the town itself was a place where all were welcome, where all could go to be whatever they sought to be, not what they *ought* to be.

Townspeople of all shapes and sizes could be found admiring the great green pine tree rising from the square, transporting fresh provisions to the quaint and toasty shops by means of cheery horse-drawn carriages, or conversing in that friendly Cobbletonian way that was always warm with kinship and connection, no matter the constant fume of breath in the chill air. Chuckling children often raced along the pavements of the charmingly narrow and crooked streets, maneuvering around lampposts and passersby as they followed ribbons of magic that streamed through the air like fireflies, a magic only they could see. Usually, it led straight to Jangles and Things, a large shop painted a merry baby blue, its marquee butter-yellow with its name printed in sprawling letters, which was rife with more than just magic, but also love.

Inside, beyond the jingle of the bell above the door, it was bright, colorful, and lively. The magnificent clock that chimed in the second-story window drew in children and adults alike, who delighted in its one-of-a-kind games, gadgets, and gizmos that gyrated, twirled, and flew around the vast space. If the coldness in the frozen town wasn't enough to take one's breath away, Jangles and Things always delivered. The whole shop was abuzz. Customers, gasping and giggling, crossed the checkerboard tiles to marvel at the emporium. Everything was alive, even things that shouldn't have been. Hot-air balloons floated through the shop like jolly, lollipop-colored lanterns. Bejeweled birds and beetles chirped from within gilded cages. Cats fashioned from plates of brass purred sweetly. Painted seagulls and clouds drifted by overhead on invisible cables. Ferris-wheel-like contraptions crammed with sweets rotated seemingly of their own accord. Dolls, toys, and games unraveled from every nook and cranny, full of promise and surprise.

The shop truly lived up to its nickname: World of Wishes and Wonder.

While guests enjoyed the sprawling ground floor with its plentiful potential presents, and its chalkboards encouraging customers to buy one thing, then another, there was an upper-level landing, reachable by way of a grand mahogany staircase or the sliding ladders that glided along the shop's shelves. Some claimed to have seen the shop owner flitting past the door above, when he wasn't holed up in his secret workshop. Curious crowds flocked from all around, hoping for a look at the many new and whimsical toys, but also for a glimpse of the greatest inventor of all . . .

Jeronicus Jangle.

Jangles and Things was a marvel indeed,

inspiring to all—and to none more than

Jeronicus's trusted apprentice, Gustafson . . .

Chapter Two

In the comfortable warmth of Jangles and Things, Gustafson captivated a crowd of inquisitive customers with his peculiar prototype of a winged wooden toy.

Despite his snug and shabby waistcoat, oversized striped shirt, and soiled newsboy hat, the young fellow was a true showman—or at least possessed the early markings of one. “Prepare yourself for Gustafson’s magnificent—!” He flashed an enthusiastic grin. “Marvelous—!” he continued, unable to contain his excitement. “Bout of brilliance!” He waggled his finger for effect. “The Twirling . . .” He spun in a circle, much to the enjoyment of the engrossed onlookers. “Whirly!”

The little crowd watched in awe and anticipation as Gustafson set his invention down on a table, and although he gestured for them to give him space, they hemmed in around him all the same, trying to get a better look.

Gustafson wound a key sticking out the top of the prototype, twisting it and twisting it with a clicking and a clattering of tiny gears.

The toy's wooden fins turned up and began to spin like an airplane propeller.

The onlookers erupted in cheers as it hovered in the air, and Gustafson's face broke into a satisfied grin. The twirling invention pulled the attention of all in the shop, including that of the owner's wife, Joanne Jangle, who looked lovely with her corkscrew curls spiraling alongside an elegant braid, and wore lemon-yellow skirts and a cherry-red jumper. She stopped ringing up a customer at the wooden cash register to point out the miraculous toy to them.

Just then, the Twirling Whirly came crashing down.

It shattered into bits of cogs and coils!

Startled and shocked reactions quickly morphed into mocking ones as customers laughed and pointed at Gustafson, who removed his hat and nervously wrung it.

"Come on! It works! It— It really does! Just a few tweaks, that's all!" he stammered.

Gustafson *fancied* himself a great inventor. But that distinction had *already* been taken by the famous shop owner, whose whimsical *working* toys drew away Gustafson's deserters.

There, above, on the upper-level landing festooned with ribbons and wreaths, the doors flew open, and out stepped Jeronicus Jangle, the most wondrous man in all the land. He was handsome with twinkling brown eyes and black hair cut in a short wave with a side part, and he was dressed in a mustard-yellow tartan suit, bow tie, and blue waistcoat. Children flew up the staircase and greeted him, singing his praises as he doled out toys. Once they'd scurried back downstairs, he clasped his hands together, sighed contentedly, then smiled as he contemplated the possibilities that the day ahead had to offer. From the moment he woke up, his mind never stopped spinning.

"Package for Jeronicus Jangle!" a mail courier called from the doorway.

The smile vanished from Jeronicus's face. In the next instant, he was flying down the steps, gliding across the checkerboard floor, and closing his fingers around the cylindrical parcel in the courier's outstretched hands. As the courier turned to leave, Jeronicus's heart began to race.

"Is this . . . ?" He inspected the package addressed to him, then beamed. "It is!" He whirled around and showed the package to Joanne. From behind the register, her eyes went wide.

In that instant, they knew nothing was going to be the same ever again.

Joanne and Jeronicus climbed the stairs to the upper-level landing, where Joanne held the parcel as he slid its casing away to reveal a thick cannister with ornate flourishes carved at either end. Embossed in the middle were the words **FINAL INGREDIENT OF THE INVENTION**. He set it down with great care on a rickety table.

All their lives they'd waited for this day.

Returning to the floor below, Jeronicus hopped onto the countertop to address his customers, overcome by the Christmas spirit deep in his soul. "I am giving it all away. It's your lucky day!"

The crowd went wild. It was a wondrous sound Gustafson wished had been for his behalf, and he momentarily forgot about trying to get Jeronicus's attention to help him troubleshoot his busted prototype. As if it wasn't bad enough that Gustafson was Jeronicus's apprentice and aspiring inventor, he also lived in and tended to the shop as his assistant.

Gustafson's jaw dropped—not only was Jeronicus the greatest inventor, but also the most generous. It was a concept he found difficult to fathom, and a reminder of his own shortcomings.

Joanne hoisted a large patchwork sack onto the countertop, and Jeronicus immediately reached in and tossed toys around the room—everything from nutcrackers and number puzzles to firecrackers and flutes. Customers rejoiced and thanked him for his grand show of kindness.

"It's going to be a merry, merry Christmas indeed!" Jeronicus exclaimed.

Basket in hand, Joanne burst out on the snowy cobblestone street and gave away gadgets and gizmos to the townspeople. Jeronicus joined her and procured even more toys from their patchwork bag to distribute. It was a display of goodwill that had never before graced the cobblestones of Chancer Street.

A little girl rounded the corner and emerged onto the busy lane. She was bright-eyed and smiling, looking cute as a cog in a cranberry dress, with the teeth of decorative gears pinning up her cloudlike hair, and a sleek leather-bound book of designs tucked under her arm. Jessica was a Jangle through and through. When she saw her parents dishing out gifts, her excitement intensified. She bolted to Jeronicus, who now stood in the flatbed of a horse-drawn carriage.

"Daddy! Daddy! What's going on?" Jessica called out, her eyes sparkling.

Jeronicus bent to rest his big hands on her little shoulders. "Oh, sweetie! It is the most wonderful day! Hey, remember that thing Daddy told you he was gonna get you?"

"Which thing?" Jessica asked. Could it have been her own pair of inventor goggles she'd been asking for, purple band and all? Or perhaps it was a brand-new instrument for her tool belt!

Jeronicus laughed. "It doesn't matter. I'm gonna get you ten of them!" He undid the necklace he always wore and looped it over his daughter's head before jumping off the carriage and joining Joanne by the shop.

Jessica studied the tiny invention dangling from the

necklace in her palm. It looked like a silver-and-gold whistle, and made curious clicking noises. And was it glowing?

Inspired, she hurried through the upbeat and celebratory crowd to reach her parents, whose basket and bag were now empty. Jeronicus lifted Jessica and spun her while Joanne lovingly looked on. In the next moment, Jessica was leading them back into the shop, which was now quiet, since the customers had left to follow Jeronicus and Joanne into the street. She sprinted up the staircase, eager to explore her own racing imagination.

"Jessica, wait for your father," Joanne called out, hot on her daughter's heels.

"Mom, I have to get my smock!" Jessica replied. "We're inventing!"

Before Jeronicus could reach the steps, Gustafson appeared behind him.

"Hey, hey, uh, professor, you said you'd— You promised you'd look at my invention," he said nervously, handing him the Twirling Whirly. He'd figured now was as good a time as any.

"Ooh." Jeronicus returned it to him before ascending the stairs.

Stuttering and stammering, Gustafson squeezed past him and stopped on the step above. "N-no, no, no! Professor, wait! Just a couple minutes—"

"Did you calibrate the gyroscopic stabilization system like we discussed?" Jeronicus asked jovially as he continued upward and reached the landing. If Gustafson had done that, all the Twirling Whirly needed was a gyroscopic stabilizer to get it up and running properly!

Gustafson flushed. “No, no, n-not yet, but—”

“Realign the gimbals?” Jeronicus picked up the canister containing the final ingredient for his latest life-changing invention.

Gustafson followed him onto the landing. “No, but professor—”

“You do that, and I’ll take a look at it tomorrow,” Jeronicus said from the doorway.

Gustafson held up the pieces of his invention. “Hey! But professor—!”

“Brilliance beckons! Genius awaits!” And with that, Jeronicus sprinted away, toward his secret workshop and out of sight.

Gustafson dropped his arms at his sides and sagged in defeat. Then he gazed down at the empty shop and his semblance of an invention—shattered in hand like all his dreams. What he’d give for one fraction of Jeronicus’s notoriety, or for a shop to call his own one day. He was tired of waiting for tomorrows. He was tired of living in Jeronicus’s giant warm-and-fuzzy shadow.

But what was a sad and lowly apprentice boy to do?

Inventing together as a family

was just as much a holiday tradition

for the Jangles as baking Christmas cookies.

Chapter Three

Jeronicus arrived upstairs, where a pair of bookshelf doors swung open to reveal his workshop.

Flames crackled in the hearth of the brick fireplace, and over a long worktable in the center of the room stood prototypes of his inventions among percolating vials and beakers of vibrant liquids that bubbled and steamed. Jeronicus pulled a lever, and a sled-like contraption lowered from the ceiling and stopped just above his shoulders to dress him in his leather inventor smock. He regarded the cannister in his hands with glee, then reached up and grabbed his inventor goggles as the contraption began to lift. At his worktable, he set down the tube.

"I told you he'd already be here!" came Jessica's voice. Seconds later, she and Joanne burst into the workshop while Jeronicus crossed the room to his giant book of inventions propped up on a stand. Jessica, now wearing her own inventor apron, set down her little notebook of designs and raced over to her father, who kept flipping pages. Despite his book's size, the designs drawn within were each more intricate than the last, with tiny notes and labels scribbled in the margins.

Finally, he paused on a spread marked by a blue ribbon, tapping the page with his finger.

It showed a design for a toy matador, or bullfighter. *This* figurine would be the toy that would change everything. And now, he possessed the final ingredient to make it all possible . . .

He rubbed his hands together to warm up, and Jessica mirrored his movements. It was their father-daughter tradition whenever inventing was afoot. He stopped to blow on each of his flattened palms, sending sparkles flurrying off his fingertips, and Jessica did the same. Then he scribbled formulas in the air with his finger. The mathematical notations floated before him and glowed like streaks of flaming lava. Joanne and Jessica eagerly looked on, though only Jeronicus could see the shimmering symbols. Still, Jessica traced her pointer finger through the air, copying him as he shifted around variables, coefficients, and exponents to his satisfaction.

"If my calculations are correct"—he stopped to scrutinize his formula—"this is it."

Back at his worktable, with his inventor goggles on and Joanne and Jessica flanking him, Jeronicus carefully took up the ornate cannister and flipped it open. Inside lay a smaller, thinner cannister, which opened to reveal an even tinier one nestled inside, which opened to reveal the final ingredient to create the matador, the toy he'd been dreaming of inventing his whole life. He lifted the pointed pipette with a blue bulb at one end.

Moments later, the Jangles gathered around The Jangleator 2000, a machine with a series of tubing, pipes, and propellers. Jeronicus delicately squeezed the single gleaming blue drop from the pipette into a funneled opening. "Something should happen *now*," he said victoriously.

The Jangleator 2000 remained still. Nothing happened.

He looked at Joanne and Jessica, who looked at the machine, waiting.

"*Now*," he repeated, waving his hands over it.

Everyone held their breaths.

Suddenly, steam shot out the top of the machine!

"Now!" Jeronicus shouted and ducked down.

The machine howled like a train. Its cogs began to spin as liquids coursed through its loops of coils. The lights in the workshop sputtered. Joanne held Jessica tight as they watched.

"It's working!" Jeronicus tapped pedals, twisted wheels, cranked valves, and yanked levers. The Jangleator sparked and bucked, and Joanne gasped while Jessica tittered.

"Don't be alarmed." Jeronicus popped up from the other side of the machine. "This is how it's *supposed* to happen."

He ducked back down, and Joanne broke into laughter. Finally, with one last twist of a wheel, and a pleased shout, the whistling machine quieted. Everyone leaned in close.

A radiant blue liquid filled a tiny glass dropper.

The recipe for the matador was complete.

Jeronicus cranked an arm of the machine, guiding its dropper over the foot-tall toy. The slender figurine wore a fitted baby-blue bolero jacket with intricate details and a corbatín, and had a head of jet-black hair with a mustache and goatee. He was slumped over. A minuscule funnel jutted out from the place where a spine should have been. Jeronicus directed the drop into it.

Then the toy began to straighten and stretch.

Everyone crouched down around the matador, who stood on a little round pedestal. He began to hum. When he realized he had an audience, he cleared his throat and struck a dashing pose with the grace of a flamenco dancer. "¡Olé! It is I, Maestro Don Juan Diego!" he said. "When the bull sees me, he slays himself. It is an *honor* for *you* to finally meet *me*." He bowed low to the admiring Jangles.

"And I-I'm Jeronicus." Jeronicus bowed in turn, but not nearly as elegantly as Don Juan. So overcome by his emotions, Jeronicus was nearly at a loss for words. "And this . . . *this* is my wonderful family."

"¡Hola, maravillosa familia!" Don Juan greeted.

Jeronicus picked up the pedestal on which Don Juan stood.

The matador swayed sideways, but steadied himself. "¡Cuidado! ¡Cuidado!" he urged.

"Gotcha," Jeronicus said, carrying him across the room.

"I am fragile," Don Juan reminded him. "You can throw roses at my feet."

Taking great care, Jeronicus rushed toward his work-table, with Joanne and Jessica in tow. "Look at that! Look at that!" He set the pedestal down, and he and Jessica leaned over it. "Everything we ever dreamed of," Jeronicus breathed, unable to take his eyes off the toy.

Don Juan turned to Jessica. "I like when people stare at me! I give them something to stare at! In the form of a dance!" He struck a limber stance.

Jessica mirrored his lithe movements, clearly entertained.

Jeronicus took Joanne's hands in his. "Everything I ever promised you will be ours now." They could afford to keep the shop for years to come, to purchase a house high on the bluffs!

"I believe in you, Jeronicus," Joanne said.

"Hello!" Don Juan chimed in. "Magical toy just come to life! Focus. Focus!"

Jessica rested a hand on Jeronicus's arm. "I believe in you the most."

"Aww, I cry," Don Juan butted in.

Jeronicus stooped down so that he and Jessica were eye level. "And I believe in you." He pinched her chin. "That's why"—he jubilantly stepped to a cluttered desk, where he opened a simple wooden box and pulled out a pair of shiny gold inventor goggles—"I got *you* an early Christmas gift." He presented the goggles to her, with a purple band, just like she'd wanted.

She cradled them in her hands as if they were baby birds. "My own inventor goggles! They're perfect!" She enveloped her father in the biggest hug.

"Now you're an inventor," he whispered.

She beamed. "Just like you."

"Aww," Don Juan said. "Okay! Back to me!"

From the doorway, Gustafson had heard the heartfelt exchange. He yearned for that sort of recognition and approval as an inventor, and something else—the love of his own family. He glanced down at his shoddy prototype in hand. Then his sights landed on Don Juan, his eyes widening in amazement. "Professor . . . professor, you did it!" he said, rushing over and crouching down at the table to admire the breathing, living matador toy. "B-but . . . how?"

"¡Ay! ¡Dios mío!" Don Juan regarded Gustafson. "You are very stinky!"

Jeronicus, Joanne, and Jessica started at his arrival. Then again, the workshop doubled as his room, with a loft bed against a far wall, so his showing up was a very common occurrence.

But never had Gustafson seen such an uncommon toy,

not in all his many years of living there, in that very room. He still couldn't believe his eyes at the miraculous feat. "He's perfect!"

Don Juan brushed off Gustafson's praise. "Por favor—admire me from a distance."

Jessica giggled.

"And soon, there'll be a million of him," Jeronicus shared in a dreamy voice.

Don Juan's green eyes bugged. "A million of *me*?" He gulped.

"One for every child in the world."

Don Juan shook his head. "But I . . . am one of a kind," he retorted.

"Jeronicus, we have to celebrate!" Joanne said. "Let me get dinner ready."

"Yes, indeed," Jeronicus replied. Before he knew it, Joanne was rushing out of the workshop to prepare dinner, with Jessica skipping behind her.

"Excuse me! Wonderful family!" Don Juan was still stuck on the idea of being replicated.

Jeronicus untied his smock and placed it over his apprentice. "Gustafson, straighten up everything for me. And take good care of our new friend." He wore a look of utmost wonder.

The toy gave him an upbeat thumbs-up in turn. "¡Señor!"

"Whose very existence has changed everything," Jeronicus concluded.

Don Juan dipped his head. "I would like to discuss this *million* thing."

"Jeronicus!" Jessica called. The smell of cinnamon and mulling spices wafted up the stairs.

"I'll be right there, my love!" Jeronicus hurried out the doors.

"Oh, professor! Yoo-hoo!" Don Juan yelled, vying for his attention.

Gustafson held up his prototype. "Oh! Wait! But would you look at my invention—"

"It's gonna be a merry Christmas!" Jeronicus shouted to the rafters. "Wait till Delacroix sees this! We'll finally be able to pay back the bank! A merry Christmas indeed!" He began his descent down the spiral staircase until his footfalls faded away to nothing.

But it wouldn't be a merry Christmas.

Not if Gustafson could help it . . .

GUSTAFSON HAD BEEN WILLING TO DO WHATEVER IT WOULD

TAKE TO ACHIEVE A BETTER LIFE FOR HIMSELF,

EVEN IF IT MEANT RESORTING TO

FECKLESS TREACHERY

AND DECEIT.

Chapter Four

"I'm an inventor, too," Gustafson muttered once he was alone—well, not entirely alone.

From the worktable, Don Juan watched the young man with a sudden interest. "Clearly not a good one," he muttered. "Stinky? Yes. Good? No." He cackled sadly. "A million of me?"

"'Calibrate the gyroscopic stabilization system,'" Gustafson babbled, removing the smock and climbing onto the sunken mattress of his loft bed. "'Realign the gimbals.' It's all he has to say to me!" He set down his fractured Twirling Whirly, lay back, and gazed up at the ceiling. He *always* helped with Jeronicus's inventions whenever he had the chance, but felt Jeronicus never really helped with his.

At least, not as soon and as easily as Gustafson craved. "I know stuff." He stared long and hard at his prototype.

Why had it malfunctioned? What in the world was the matter with him?!

"Who could conceive of such a thing? This is absurd!" Don Juan leaped off his little pedestal and loped across the surface with smoking flasks, steaming beakers, and lustrous cogs and coils. "I am singular! I am spectacular! To pull off such a feat, you'd need—" He froze when he saw a particular page in Jeronicus's book of inventions, of a toy sketched with fine precision.

The matador quaked. "'Plans for Don Juan Doll.' ¡No puedo!" He couldn't bear the thought of being mass-produced. If only he could figure out a way to remain one of a kind. Suddenly, Don Juan had an idea. A smug smile twisted his handsome features as he glanced at Gustafson. Unaware of being observed, Gustafson continued to trifle with his prototype until the wrench he'd been using to tighten a screw jammed against his fingers. Recoiling in sharp pain, Gustafson dropped back on his bed and shook out his hand. Nothing ever seemed to go his way.

Unless, of course, Don Juan could offer up a new possibility for the young inventor. He seized the opportunity. "It must feel good to be such an *integral* part of bringing something so amazing to life." Don Juan nonchalantly gazed down his nose at his pristine plastic fingernails.

Gustafson was startled, having forgotten he wasn't alone. "It was, uh, it was the professor's work, really."

He resumed fiddling with his prototype. "I'm just his apprentice," he added sadly.

Don Juan coyly swept his spotless black shoe back and forth across the tabletop. "Sí, pero I am sure you've created something of your own, almost as amazing as me. After all, you're an inventor, too." He was playing right into Gustafson's glaring insecurity. He waited for a reply.

Gustafson stopped tinkering and looked up. Could it be? Someone else who recognized his budding brilliance and maturing magnificence? He regarded his Twirling Whirly, grimacing, and set it back down before springing from his bed and taking up a broom to sweep. "I'm telling everyone just a few tweaks are all it needs. But the professor always promises to look at it tomorrow."

"The bull waits for tomorrow! But by then he is dead!" Don Juan's subdued tone was gone, replaced by a voice full of intensity. "*We* wait for no tomorrows!"

Gustafson stopped sweeping. What was the toy matador talking about?

Don Juan gestured to the book of inventions. "That can belong to us," he tempted.

"Those are the professor's inventions," Gustafson retorted with a finger wag.

"*Those* are *your* inventions!" Don Juan declared. "Those pages bear the sweat of your fingers. They're as much yours as they are his."

"But that would be stealing."

"Borrowing. Indefinitely," Don Juan corrected. It was an odd turn of phrase, but still . . .

"Together, we can build an empire," Don Juan continued with vigor. "The name Gustafson will shine brighter than a thousand Spanish skies. And I, Don Juan Diego, will remain one, and only one, of a kind. It's easy . . . It's not stealing . . . when you borrow *indefinitely* . . ."

Gustafson's eyes flitted back to the massive book, which beckoned to him with its hundreds of pages of designs. As he thought about ditching his days of incessant tinkering and tidying for the life of fame and fortune promised in every page, the corner of his mouth crept upward. It would be so easy. An entire, brilliant future was just within his grasp . . .

Jeronicus, trusting and true,

always saw the best in people—

especially those whom he held near.

But a biting wind of change blew from on high that

would sweep aside all he held dear . . .

Chapter Five

"Gustafson! You didn't think we'd have a family celebration without you, did you?"

Jeronicus came barreling up the spiral staircase, balancing a tray of honey-dipped ham, mashed potatoes, and for dessert, sugar biscuits and cranberry juice—Gustafson's favorites.

There was also a tiny wrapped box resting on the tray with an early Christmas gift inside: the gyroscopic stabilizer needed to doctor the Twirling Whirly.

"Answer soon, or this food will find a happy home in my belly!" Jeronicus gave a hearty laugh. "Gustafson!" When he stepped foot in his workshop, his apprentice was no longer there.

Jeronicus scanned the room once more, his smile flagging.

There was Don Juan's pedestal—minus Don Juan.

There was his wooden book stand—minus his book.

The abstraction of the subtraction meant he could only deduce one common denominator.

Jeronicus's smile fell, and he staggered dizzily. His tray crashed to the floor, its contents clattering. How could this be? Had someone he deeply trusted and cared for, someone he'd housed and fed and taught, someone whom he considered family, truly just betrayed his trust?

Jeronicus raced back downstairs, calling out for Gustafson. He burst into the cold street. It was dark, save for coal fires and slanted shapes of light streaming softly from shop windows.

"Gustafson!" he cried again and again.

But his voice was only lost to howling winds and distant carolers. He peered through the window of Sisson Arms, the pub next door, thinking maybe Gustafson had gone there for a cup of hot cocoa. But he was not there. Horror gripped Jeronicus, closing around his heart, tightening his throat. He dashed down the lane, where a horse pulled a Gustafson-less carriage around the bend.

"Gustafson!" Jeronicus ran frantically back to the front of his shop, where he let out a strangled sob. His plans to replicate Don Juan had been stolen from him, along with his sacred book of designs that not only secured his family's future, but also the joy born from his toys and trinkets for tots, tweens, teens, and all who needed it. For years, he and his family had worked hard to get to where they were, from their days peddling their wares at a makeshift trolley in the square to the day they earned a store to call their own. He and Joanne had talked at length about paying off the debt on the shop, with enough profits to afford their dream home, and even a good school for Jessica where she could prosper. But now, all those plans had been snuffed out.

How could Gustafson have deceived them?

Joanne and Jessica appeared in the doorway, holding each other.

With heaving breaths, Jeronicus stared into the night as it began to snow—the first flakes before everything would snowball.

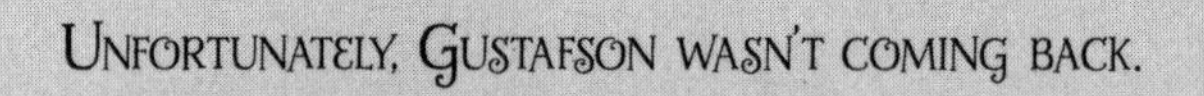

Unfortunately, Gustafson wasn't coming back.

Not then . . . or perhaps ever.

Chapter Six

Jeronicus tried to convince the constable of what Gustafson had done, but he had no proof. And so, in the coming weeks and months, Jeronicus, ever the optimist, returned to what he knew best.

Day in and day out, he didn't shy away from finessing prototypes in his workshop. Only . . . things weren't quite the same. He couldn't seem to find the right screw, or turn the right gear.

And year after year, the the crowds shrunk and the bills stacked high while his once-trusted apprentice emerged as the world's biggest toy maker. The chuckling children on Chancer Street played with gadgets and gizmos with a *G* emblazoned on each, a constant reminder of Gustafson's presence. Only the Jangles knew the truth: Gustafon's toys were each based on Jeronicus's ingenious designs in his stolen book of inventions (though the world had yet to see Don Juan dolls, meaning the matador must have gotten his wish of remaining one of a kind). It was worse than seeing the factory that Gustafson had built on the craggy bluffs overlooking the town, its gigantic *G* shining bright as a beacon and as green as the exact shade of jealousy.

Still, Jeronicus was determined. Once a great inventor, always a great inventor. He kept at ideating, working his hands to the bone. Eventually, when he tried to ignite his fiery formulas in the air, they flickered, and went out. Despite his faltering, Joanne and Jessica continued to support him and his ever-creative endeavors, along with his banker and friend, Mr. Delacroix, who'd wish him words of encouragement. But the magic, it seemed, had escaped him.

And soon, so would everything else.

One day, Joanne collapsed in his arms outside the shop, dropping a bag of groceries brimming with fresh-cut flowers. He rushed her to her bed, where he held a warm cloth to her forehead. She had taken ill. Jessica watched from the doorway. She had only ever seen her mother brave, beautiful, and strong. But Joanne faded, shrinking, until one night, she was gone.

The funeral came and went like a biting winter wind. The engraving on the headstone was forever etched in Jeronicus's and Jessica's minds, solidifying their bleak new reality.

JOANNE JANGLE

BELOVED WIFE AND MOTHER

Jeronicus was devastated. Jessica tried to fill the space left behind, but the loss was too great, and Jessica too small. Her hot meals for Jeronicus grew cold on the worktable. Her visits happened less and less as her father's inventions and boxes piled up around him, dust coating every inch of the workshop. Sheets covered inventions as they would a corpse. Jessica had only ever seen her father cheerful and upbeat, but the sunny sparkle in his eyes had dimmed to a faint flicker, blinding him to her love, and his moods became brooding, mercurial.

Eventually, Jessica could stand it no longer for it was clear she hadn't lost just one parent, but two.

One day, once she'd grown, the time came for Jessica to leave home. Suitcase in hand, she climbed into a carriage, where she stared out the back. Her eyes welled with tears as she watched the shop—the only home she'd ever known—fade away.

And Jangles and Things, once a world of wishes and wonder, was no more.

And Jeronicus Jangle,

once the greatest inventor of all,

vowed never to invent anything ever again.

Chapter Seven

By looking at Pawnbroker, it was hard to imagine the thriving toy shop as it had once been.

Thirty years had eroded the marquee into a sickly, sunburnt hue, and filled the shop with the dust and darkness that comes in the wake of any devastation. Gone was the World of Wishes and Wonder—in its place clung a world of woes and worries. Languishing furniture and junk with grimy numbered placards littered the cobwebbed nooks and crannies. Items for buying or selling included the likes of broken bicycles, crooked chairs, cracked sleds, and upright pianos missing a few keys. One sign threatened **NO REFUNDS, NO EXCHANGES, NO NOTHING**. The cold freeze of Cobbleton had won out, seeping into every inch of the shop down to its splinters.

And Jeronicus, like the shop's rubbish, had become a thing in need of mending. Old and hunched, he wore a shabby patchwork waistcoat over a ratty shirt. His black beard hid most of his face, which had fallen into disrepair, with frown lines where smile lines once lived. The hair on the top of his head had grayed. He sat staring at a cuckoo clock through his thick magnifying glass, examining its elegantly carved case. He'd have to take it apart and put it back together again.

"The cuckoo inside just doesn't cuckoo," said the customer sadly, looking aristocratic in a dark purple dress and green feathered hat. "It's a bit of a family heirloom. Do you have family?"

The question struck a nerve with Jeronicus, who shifted in his chair.

A loud *crash* shook him from his thoughts.

"I'm okay! I'm okay!" a squeaky voice piped in. There was another loud *bang*, and a boy appeared from behind a stack of old travel trunks and a fringed lamp. He had his curly black hair parted in the center, a green polka-dot bow tie, owlish eyeglasses, and a sheepish toothy expression.

He approached the counter with a mop in his hand. "I've swept the shop, wiped down the counters, and mopped the floor," he said in a self-satisfied manner, resting the mop against the counter beside Jeronicus, who didn't bother looking up at him, wiry glasses fixed on the cuckoo.

"Did you clean the pantry?" Jeronicus asked.

"Ugh!" his apprentice sighed. He'd forgotten. He'd do better.

The lady turned her attention back to Jeronicus. "It would mean a lot if you could fix it."

Jeronicus peered down at the clock's hopelessly rotten bellows.

"Of *course* he can fix it!" the boy chimed in. "I mean, he's the greatest inventor of all," he said, flashing Jeronicus a look of admiration.

"Children," Jeronicus mumbled dismissively. "Active imaginations."

The boy reached for a tool on the counter, and Jeronicus swatted his hand.

"I'll give you half a crown for it," Jeronicus said to the lady.

She nodded, pleased.

"After he fixes it, it'll be worth *ten* pounds. Or even a *hundred*!" the boy declared with a defensive shake of his head. He refused to let Jeronicus sell himself short.

Soon, the boy saw the customer out. "Bye!" he buoyantly called, waving from the door.

From down the busy lane, a stern voice called out: "Edison! Time for your chores!"

The boy opened the door wider and craned his neck out. "Mom! We're *inventing*!"

Jeronicus appeared behind him. "This is a *pawnshop*," he corrected, handing Edison his coat before steering him out of the shop. "What *don't* you understand about that?"

Edison looked wistful. "No, it's not! It's a magical, mystical—"

"Goodbye, Edison." Jeronicus shut the door in his face. There was no longer room in his life for exuberance—only exasperation. The rusty bell above the door jangled as if in agreement.

That didn't stop Edison from continuing to speak to him, even if it was through one of the frosted shop windows. "World of Wishes and Wonder!" Edison concluded jubilantly.

But Jeronicus had left that world behind long, long ago.

Like the silent bird stuck in the cuckoo clock,

Jeronicus felt his singing days were also over.

Chapter Eight

"Good morning, Edison!" the local postal woman called out happily. "Invent anything today?"

"Not yet!" he replied as he ran past her.

She looked gorgeous in her red cloak and luxurious black hair tucked and pinned neatly under a flat-brimmed hat, and her heart was as big as the giant bag of mail she had slung over her shoulder. She strolled through the street, pushing her mail trolley with its large wicker basket.

Around her, Cobbleton was aflutter. Townspeople finished hanging the star on top of the evergreen that stood like a lonely sentinel in the square. Everyone was bustling to and fro, lunching or shopping for Christmas, which was in a few days' time. Ms. Johnston abandoned her mail trolley and marched straight for the pawnshop. She stopped and took a moment to collect herself before she turned the corner and pushed open its double doors. Jeronicus, still tinkering on the cuckoo clock at the counter, barely registered her. She turned and clamorously attempted to shut the doors behind her before taking a deep breath and spinning excitedly back to face Jeronicus.

He stood. “Good morning, Mrs. Johnston,” he said with the semblance of a smile.

She twirled her midnight-blue skirts. “Good morning, Jerry.” She took a few steps into the silent, squalid shop as Jeronicus sat back down. “It’s so dark in here,” she remarked. She hit buttons, one by one, on a switchboard, and sconces and chandeliers flared to life, much to Jeronicus’s chagrin. Ms. Johnston rejoiced. “Perfect!”

“I kind of liked it the way it was,” Jeronicus told her matter-of-factly.

Ignoring the comment, she sauntered up to him. “How’s my favorite pawnbroker? Hmm? Who’s not really a pawnbroker but wants everyone to believe he is? Hmm?” she teased. “Jerry?”

He set down the cuckoo. “I’d be better if you called me by my name.”

She lifted a defunct telephone and spoke into it in a low, sultry tone. “Hello, Jerry.”

“It’s Jeronicus,” he corrected, but not unkindly.

“It’s *Jerry*!” she sang with a playful wink.

Jeronicus blinked again. “You have something for me today, Mrs. Johnston?”

She scowled and leaned over the countertop. "It's *Ms.* I'm widowed, remember? He's dead. Gone. Ain't never coming back."

Jeronicus looked up at her. "I'm sure he's in a better place."

"Jerry the Jokester." She fished a letter out of her mailbag and handed it to him. "Here. You might want to open this one. You're three months late on your gas. Actually, it's four, but you overpaid the month before, so they gave you a credit." She dangled the letter in front of him.

When he reached for it, she yanked it back a few times until he managed to grab it.

"Mrs. Johnston, I would appreciate it—"

"*Ms.*," she interjected.

"If you refrained from opening my mail," Jeronicus concluded. He opened the letter and considered it for a glum moment before stashing the overdue bill into a jumbled letter drawer.

She feigned surprise. "It's just a sixth sense I have." She extended another few letters for Jeronicus. "A gift . . . knowing what's inside . . . without seeing it," she proclaimed, jerking the letters away every time Jeronicus reached for them, until finally he seized them. This time, she held tight and began giggling. Finally, she let go, and he fell backward in his chair, dropping the letters, knocking over Edison's mop, and falling against an archaic grandfather clock whose pendulum no longer swung, succumbed to a timeless existence.

He straightened. "Mrs. Johnston, I don't have time for this today."

She rolled her eyes in exasperation. "Jerry!" she growled. "Lighten up! You've just got to smile."

Jeronicus did his best to ignore her, but when he wiped off the counter with a rag, Ms. Johnston rang its little bell, jarring his senses. And when he crossed the floor to buff an antique violin with snapped and fraying strings, Ms. Johnston followed like a relentless shadow. She knew Jeronicus was down on his luck ever since he lost Joanne to her sickness, and since Jessica packed up and left home. But she also knew that there was still hope for him to be happy again, maybe with someone like her by his side to let in some light. She glided on a tall ladder.

He shook his head at her behavior. "You do realize people can see you from outside."

She leaned close to him, fluttering her eyelashes.

Just then, a man burst into the shop, looking prim and proper in a dark blue cloak and top hat with a burnt-orange waistcoat and gray muttonchops connected by a thick mustache. He regarded Ms. Johnston.

"Mrs. Johnston was just . . ." Jeronicus made to move away from her. "Delivering the mail."

Ms. Johnston sighed and spun away from him. She dug into her mailbag and handed a letter to the man. "You know, your cousin is visiting for the holidays," she told him. "Merry Christmas." She reached the double doors.

"Hopefully my favorite cousin," the man mused, eyeing the letter.

Ms. Johnston twirled back around. "Nope." And with that, she left.

The man flipped the letter over, seeing that it was indeed sealed.

"Mr. Delacroix," Jeronicus said, drawing his attention.

The banker regarded him with tenderness. "Jangle."

Jeronicus crossed to a tiny table. "Just the person I've been waiting for."

Mr. Delacroix followed close behind. "Yes. Which is why you haven't answered any of my inquiries." His voice dripped with sarcasm, despite being one of Jeronicus's biggest believers.

Jeronicus gulped. "Yes, I've been thinking—"

"Jangle," Mr. Delacroix cut in, loosening the cuffs of his jacket, "for the last thirty years you've been promising something sensational."

"Yes. And I have a thought," Jeronicus said with a nervous little chuckle.

"Yes! Something *spectacular*," Mr. Delacroix stated.

Jeronicus picked an empty gravy boat off the table. "Silver."

Mr. Delacroix sighed. *This* was what he'd had in mind?

"You melt it down," Jeronicus continued. "It's a three-point-five. It'll be a four-point-five next year—"

"Something *stupendous*," Mr. Delacroix cut in. "Something that will show the bank they've made a return on their investment."

"Which is why I need more time." He began flipping madly through a book. "Look, I can show you—"

"I'm sorry, Jangle," the banker said, "the bank can't wait any longer."

Jeronicus kept flipping. "Just take a quick look—"

Mr. Delacroix stuck a hand in the book to stop him. "Jeronicus, listen to me! Either come up with the money you've borrowed by Christmas—"

"Which is just a few days away," Jeronicus griped.

"Or show me the revolutionary invention you once promised," he finished.

Jeronicus racked his cobwebbed mind. "Something revolutionary?"

Mr. Delacroix nodded curtly.

Jeronicus thrust an old domed adding machine onto the counter and his once-skilled fingers punched the keys. "Take the circumference of spectacular . . . divided by the second derivative of sensational." He hit a final key, and the machine printed out a little square of paper. "It'll take approximately . . ."

Mr. Delacroix snatched the page and read it, his bushy brows vanishing into his deepening wrinkles. He let out an unamused exhale and handed the paper back to Jeronicus. "Two thousand years?" he asked skeptically.

"That may be a miscalibration on my part," Jeronicus excused.

Mr. Delacroix turned and strode away from him. "The invention, or the bank will seize Pawnbroker and all its assets," he warned.

"Wait!" Jeronicus followed on his heels. "Mr. Delacroix!"

Mr. Delacroix paused in the doorway to humor him.

Jeronicus raised his hands in surrender. "I would lose everything," he pleaded.

"I'm sorry to say it, old friend"—he looked around at the scattered shop—"but it looks like you already have." His eyes settled sadly back on Jeronicus. "Merry Christmas." And with that, he was gone.

"Merry Christmas." Jeronicus's lip trembled as he dissolved to tears. He had to think. He had to do something. He felt as off-kilter as his shop. It was all he had left. It may have changed, but it was still filled with so many fuzzy memories of his wife and his daughter and his delighted customers. "Something revolutionary . . ." he mused. "Something revolutionary . . ."

Within moments, he was padding up the spiral staircase to his secret workshop. He slid a trunk out from under a desk and hoisted it up. It was a dusty old travel trunk, one painted with flowers and stickered with papers from around the globe. He traced his fingers along the stickers before taking a deep breath and creaking open the lid. There he found, buried among knickknacks and scrolls of paper, a sleek red notebook. The letters **JESSICA J** printed on the front shone just as they had in Jessica's happy, cozy childhood.

He opened to the first pages of a child's doodles and found words like **EXPLORE** and **TRUTH** and **LOVE** and **FOCUS**, and there was a crayon-drawn Jangles and Things with the phrase **THE MOST MAGICAL SHOP IN THE WORLD**. There were even stick figures of the three of them together.

What he'd give to go back in time, to cherish those moments once more.

He turned to a page marked by a glossy red ribbon. It showed the designs of a smiling robot with giant eyes and a cherubic face: **THE BUDDY 3000**. His fingers grazed the illustration.

The shadow of a long-lost smile twitched across Jeronicus's lips.

Then, something else in the trunk caught his eye, something small wrapped in a soft brown cloth. He removed the fabric to reveal a dusty glass cube with a gold-trimmed door. Through it, he saw dozens of little gears angled in every direction. He used his sleeve to lovingly polish it.

"There you are," he breathed.

Could this robot be his something revolutionary?

He may have found the one thing to change everything,

but still, something was missing.

Someone was missing . . .

Over the years, Jessica sifted through mail, searching for a letter from her father.

Many times he sat to write. And though she had moved far away, the heart, it seems, isn't bothered by distance. Only by what it loves and wishes loved it in return.

But Jeronicus couldn't figure out the words.

Perhaps *I'm sorry* hadn't quite been invented yet. And Jessica, lowering the mail onto her desk one cold gray day, grew weary of the wait. She had a life of her own now. And a daughter—a peculiar little girl. Curious. Magical, even, some might say . . .

Journey Jangle.

Chapter Nine

Woodsmoke trailed out the chimney of Nesbitt Cottage on a pale morning much like any other.

The little home and its snowy square yard were hemmed in by hedges and a wrought iron fence crystallized in ice. Inside, Journey was hard at work on her latest invention—a bird automaton. The little girl reached for a piece of wood resting on her desk. She wore a blue ribbon studded with cogs in her puffy black hair, a leather tool belt looped around her shoulders, and a rainbow jumper with whimsical ruffled shoulders. If the details of her appearance didn't give her away as an innovator, the pages of designs papered around her bedroom certainly did. Journey was an inventor, like the grandfather she'd never known but had only ever heard so much about, including his magnificent shop, his whimsical inventions, and his ability to see things . . .

Journey may have been small, but she had big, brilliant ideas and a brave, mighty heart.

She measured the wood, chiseled out a piece, and fit it onto her bird automaton. Then she checked her pages of designs in her notebook. Content, she pulled the piece of wood, which made the bird's wings move up and down. She wrote a line in her notebook, and stood to look out the fogged glass of her window. Like her bird creation, she, too, was born to spread her wings and fly. She'd longed to make the trip to meet her legendary grandfather. Her mother had promised that one day they'd visit Jangles and Things, but if, and only if, they were invited.

Then, one day . . .

Journey spun around as the door opened, and Jessica stood there clutching a letter. Jessica was older now, with her hair in a long, luxurious side braid, and adorned with decorative cogs on top, a nod to her creative childhood. But like her notebook that she'd put away long ago, a nod was all she had left. Well, not all. Her daughter was just as bright-eyed and optimistic as she had been once. Journey grinned at her from ear to ear.

Moments later, their boots crunched across their front yard, Journey bundled up in a royal-purple jacket with cogs stitched to the lapel and carrying a striped backpack of her scant belongings.

"It's only a couple of days," Jessica told her. "So remember to mind your manners and eat your dinner. All of it. No matter how it tastes." At the gate, she took Journey's hands, crouching down. "And be kind to your grandfather. Even if he isn't everything you've imagined he'll be."

Journey's eyes shone. "He'll be more. I just know it." She beamed.

Jessica sighed. Although Jessica wouldn't be going to see Jeronicus herself, she was still nervous, and wondered if it was a mistake to be letting Journey visit him on her own. In all those years, he'd only sent one letter. Well, even if he hadn't measured up as a father, perhaps there would still be hope for him as a grandfather. She quickly dashed her worried expression, straightened, and pulled from her sleeve an envelope addressed to Jeronicus. "Now, remember when you get to Cobbleton—"

"Mom!" Journey cut in. "I got it," she reassured her, accepting the letter.

"All aboard!" the driver shouted from the horse-drawn omnibus on the road.

Journey's face lit up in excitement. She couldn't wait!

She was going to live up to her name—a most magical journey was about to begin.

Jessica pulled her in for a hug smelling of chamomile and cocoa butter.

"I love you, Mom." Journey squeezed her tighter.

Jessica kissed her forehead. "I love you more."

The two large horses neighed impatiently, breaking their moment.

Arms flailing, Journey rushed to the road. "Wait up! I'm coming!"

Jessica watched with a heavy heart as Journey climbed into the carriage and waved through the window. Waving back, Jessica watched the carriage roll off down the pine-lined road, praying her father would know that she had sent Journey to him with love. Maybe Journey would be able to bond with him over their shared magical ability, or, with any luck, bring his smile back, the one he'd lost long ago. She pulled a necklace out of her red dress and cradled it in her hand. She kept it, all those years later, right above her heart. It still ticked and glowed, a reminder of her father, of the happy life she'd once known.

From the omnibus, Journey gazed at the passing landscape. While most little girls her age had visions of sugarplums dancing in their heads this time of year, she had equations and formulas buffeting around instead—and butterflies. She was overjoyed to visit her grandfather at long last, even if it was only for a short time. It would be a nice change from a town where people stuck up their nose at her for being different, or mocked her for the color of her skin, or for the kinks and cogs in her hair, or for her notebook full of strange and wonderful things that mattered. It would be nice to be someplace she felt like she belonged for once. She hoped, more than being able to confirm if they were as similar as her mother had always noted, more than meeting her grandfather who was also a great inventor, that Jeronicus would like her.

She paused her daydreams to jot fresh ideas in her notebook, inspired by the blue birds flitting by, and by the exponentially busy road, and by the people seated around her in the omnibus. When it rolled into Cobbleton, she was surprised by how quickly time had passed, and how very close her grandfather had been to her all her life. Out the window, she caught glimpses of the unfamiliar town bustling with holiday shoppers. Her heart began to soar.

Before she knew it, she was walking among the boisterous crowds, backpack slung over her shoulders, taking in the picturesque town with wide eyes, eating up the hustle and bustle.

Men tipped their hats kindly at her. Horses clomped by. People in clumps chatted and laughed on every sidewalk and curb despite the cold—people of all shapes and sizes. If it wasn't enough to get her imagination fired up, it was certainly enough to warm her heart.

She raced down the teeming street and descended a staircase leading to a gingerbread-smelling square fenced in by shops and restaurants, and boasting an enormous pine tree decked with lanterns, candy canes, and tinsel. A throng of people parted to reveal the spot where Jangles and Things was supposed to be located, per her mother's exact instructions to get safely to its 260 Chancer Street address.

Journey's heart pounded faster, and she hastened toward it, but halted.

JERONICUS JANGLE

PAWNBROKER

BEST SECONDHAND GOODS IN ALL OF

COBBLETON

BECAUSE TWO HANDS ARE BETTER THAN ONE

Her eyes flitted from the sign to the grimy windows taped with more signs. Many said **NO REFUNDS**. She blinked, beholding the faded marquee, the words for a toy emporium illegible.

She traipsed to the doors, and unhooked a sign from a knob that read **BACK IN 5 MINUTES. OR LESS. OR MORE. OR MORE OR LESS.** She hung it back up, and treaded down the icy sidewalk.

"Excuse me. Do you know where I can find Jeronicus Jangle?" Journey asked a lady.

She pointed. "He's right over there."

Thanking her, Journey cut across the lively square toward a trolley selling knickknacks, where a man in a faded blue-and-yellow tartan coat was turned away from her, inspecting the wares. She slowly approached him as he paid the vendor, and took a deep breath, bracing herself.

"Are you . . . Mr. Jangle?" she asked delicately.

"Depends on who's asking," Jeronicus said without looking at her.

She took a step closer. "I'm Journey. Your granddaughter."

"My granddaughter's name is Jackie, or something with a *U*."

Journey's resolve faltered.

Jeronicus moseyed from the stand, opening a book and then beginning to read it.

She marched after him. "It's Journey," she said softly.

"That's a *J-O-U*," he said, continuing to read. "Okay."

She reached her fingerless-gloved hand into her jacket and procured her mother's letter. "My mom told me to give this to you." She offered it to him, but he slighted her, continuing to pore over his book and mumble to himself, clearly not wanting to be bothered on his errands run.

Journey decided to take matters into her own hands. As they passed the pine tree and a little bench, she opened the envelope, unfolded the letter, and read aloud. "'Dear Father.'"

"Allegedly." Jeronicus glanced at her. They arrived at a stand where he purchased an egg.

"'I've decided to let Journey stay with you until Christmas,'" Journey continued.

Jeronicus took his egg. "Journey. That's an interesting name," he remarked.

"'She's an inquisitive girl, but well mannered.'" Journey relished that line. "'Like you said,'" she kept reading, "'it's time you both got to know each other.'"

He paid the vendor. "Did I say that? When did I say that?" he mused.

She followed as he moved back through the square, where scents of cinnamon and nutmeg (or was it warm apple pie?) mingled with the smells of cypress and woodsmoke. "'I'll be there to pick her up on Christmas morning. I hope you are well. Love . . . Jessica,'" she concluded.

Gingerly, he reached out and took the letter to read.

Journey held her breath, hoping it would soften him to her arrival.

He handed the letter back. "No." He beelined to his shop. "My granddaughter would never be allowed to visit me anyway."

Her face fell as she tailed him. "But I have nowhere else to stay."

He ignored her, reaching his shop's stoop.

She stepped in front of him. "I have nowhere else to stay!" she said again loudly.

Jeronicus brushed past her. "You can't stay here. Not now. Maybe next year. Or the year after. Maybe five or ten years from now. You know what they say about children. They're a creative vacuum." He passed through a door. "I can't have that right now," he added. "I'm working on something *private*." He shut the door on her, leaving her alone on the cold stoop.

Moments later, Journey entered the disarray of the shop, climbed the curving mahogany steps, and emerged on the upper-level landing overlooking the ground floor as Jeronicus tinkered with a glass cube at a little desk.

"Symmetry brings synchronicity." He fit a cog into the cube and twisted a screw. At the sound of Journey's clomping boots, Jeronicus turned to her. "I-I don't have time for this. Didn't you understand when we talked outside?"

She tore her sights from the ground floor and deftly slipped a photo out of her inside jacket pocket to show him.

He craned to look at it, and gave in to the urge to take it.

The black-and-white photo was faded, showing a chipper child, her inventor goggles perched atop her head like a coronet.

"Your mother," he breathed, in a state of disbelief. "She wanted her own pair of inventor goggles. 'I want a purple band, Daddy. They have to have a purple band.' And so that's what I did. Her mother thought she wasn't ready for it, but . . . I knew that she was." A nostalgic warmth filled his chest. He was remembering. The memories had been covered in so much dust, like all of his inert inventions. He took a deep breath and set down the photo. "You can stay," he said.

"Great!" Journey cheered.

"*After* you sign this." Jeronicus stood and pulled a folded sheaf of paper from an armoire. "As clauses of confidentiality to protect the specialty of the personality whose mentality transcends the continuum between fantasy and reality." He thumbed through the many panels of unfurling pages as he read, each filled with numerous lines of complicated terms.

She looked at him, eyebrow quirked, unsure what all that gobbledygook meant.

As if reading her mind, he said, "It means you don't touch, you don't move, you don't bust, you don't break, you don't take *anything* from this shop. You understand?" He held out a fluffy white-feathered quill.

She nodded. Now *that* she understood.

"Okay. Sign it right here," he instructed, putting his finger at the bottom.

Journey began to sign, but no ink flowed from the quill's tip. She tested it on her finger, to no avail. "The pen is out of ink," she reported.

"Keep going. The pen is full of ink," Jeronicus promised her.

Obeying, she tried again and signed her name, though no name appeared.

When she finished, he held the contract under a lamp. Under its glow, her signature materialized in neon-blue letters.

"Your signature's right here." He folded it up. "You signed it. You're under contract."

Journey was still too impressed by the invisible ink to care.

As her grandfather stuffed it back into the armoire, she lifted the glass cube off his desk and inspected its many gears, angled in every direction inside. "What's this?" she asked.

Jeronicus rushed to her. "It's none of your business," he

said. "It's exactly— It's none of your business. Okay?" He took it and sat back down.

Journey shrugged, unfazed, and marveled at the shop some more, seeing all its potential, and imagining what it had once been. If she listened hard enough, she could hear joy from long ago.

"You hungry?" Jeronicus asked. "I have one egg. We could split it."

Journey looked at him, mouth set in a sorry line, and shook her head. Like the shop, she could tell he had potential, too—and that he was struggling in more ways than one. He suggested she take her bag to a bed downstairs on the ground floor. She nodded then gave a sympathetic look before walking off, and Jeronicus put his head down and got back to work, tightening a tiny gear. She raced back to him and enveloped him in a giant hug. She hadn't needed a detailed design of Jeronicus to tell that he'd needed one, that he'd been missing one.

He froze. "What's . . . going on?" he asked as she nuzzled him.

Journey realized she'd needed a hug, too. Her grandfather smelled of the soothing scent of zesty oranges and argon oil. "Is it all right if I call you Grandpa Jeronicus?" she asked earnestly.

"Could you not?" he replied softly, despite the urge to submit to her endearing wish.

"I guess you're right," she agreed quietly. "Grandpa

J sounds *so* much better!" she corrected with an elated smile. She pecked him on the cheek several times, despite his insistent protests to stop, until finally she broke off and scurried to settle in. "See you soon, Grandpa J!"

Why wouldn't anyone call him by his name?

"Well, you hurry back as slowly as you can," he mumbled, though he didn't really mean it. He thought about how he hadn't had a hug from anyone since . . . When he was sure he was alone, he picked up the old photo. He couldn't take his eyes away. Journey had her mother's smile.

Finally, he lowered it again, and got back to work on his something revolutionary.

Jeronicus wasn't the only one

who needed something revolutionary.

Gustafson, too, was searching.

Driven by Don Juan's greed and thirst for power,

Gustafson's empire soared.

For nearly thirty Christmases, Gustafson unveiled one

stolen invention after the other . . .

until there were no more pages in Jeronicus's book!

Yes, and with Christmas just days away, Gustafson had

no choice but to revisit an idea of his own.

After all, he was an inventor, too . . .

Chapter Ten

The giant *G* glinted and glittered from Gustafson's Factory atop the bluffs, casting a shadow on the peaked, snow-blanketed roofs of the little shops and homes. With its steely domed turrets, spindly chimneys, and wall that segregated it from the rest of the humble town below, the building looked like more of a fortress than a factory, save for the stacks belching a dark, noxious smoke.

Inside, international toy buyers crowded into a cavernous showroom with ornate green woodwork paneling the walls, bloodred pillars, and stained glass double doors overlooking a dais with steps leading down to a floor of cold marble. The milling buyers were impatient to see what lay in wait beyond those doors. Could it be another legendary toy for boys and girls? One with the promise to rise to the top of every wish list? They practically frothed at the mouth in anticipation.

The double doors flew open and lights flicked on to

show a formidable silhouette, which spun around to reveal a man in an exquisite gold-trimmed cloak with tasseled epaulets. Every inch of his garments was made of the finest fabrics and jewels, from his waistcoat with lustrous buttons and royal-purple necktie, to his glossy top hat, which made him appear even taller. He wore rings on every finger, and clutched a staff topped by an incandescent green gem. His face sported a short, sculpted beard. Gone were the days of the lowly orphan boy in tattered rags. Gustafson had become what he'd always dreamed of being, a true showman, one of magic and mystique known throughout the world—the Magic Man G—and he was thrilled to show off what new invention he had up his emerald-green sleeve. He pulled a cloth off his latest shiny new toy.

There sat a far-improved version of the Twirling Whirly from thirty years prior—composed of finely crafted metals and precious plastics—rebranded as the Werly Twerly. It whirred, chortled, and took to the air, hovering over the wonderstruck buyers. It could sing and whistle and change directions on a dime. The buyers swarmed Gustafson on his dais, thrashing their hands and feverishly placing orders for the toy in the hundreds—no, in the *thousands*.

Suddenly, the invention smoked and sparked.

It nose-dived into the crowd, and buyers screamed, ducking and dodging, until it suction-cupped itself to an old man's cheek. Despite his shouting efforts to pry it off, it remained stuck.

"It's frying my face!" he cried.

"Somebody help that poor man!" a woman pleaded.

Some lifted him from the room as others rescinded their orders and cleared out.

"Let's get out of here!" shouted a buyer.

The sense of déjà vu turned Gustafson's stomach.

His jaw hung slackly, his brows furrowed as he looked on in horror. Not for the uncertain fate of the roughed-up buyer, but for his own future. He was starting to lose his spark, and he refused to let that happen. His days as a fool and a failure were far behind him. He'd made sure of that. But while he had become the greatest inventor that ever there was, it was a lie, for all Gustafson's inventions had been born of the stolen designs he'd indefinitely borrowed when he was just a boy. Now he'd just tried producing a Gustafson Original, and it hadn't worked. Any idea of his own was missing something. Or some*one* . . .

While the magic in Gustafson's Factory was lacking,

back at Jangles and Things,

Journey was discovering a magic of her own . . .

Chapter Eleven

Across town, night fell over Jeronicus's shop, and all at once it was cloaked in twinkling stars.

Journey burnished the bannister on the upper landing. "So, what are you working on?"

Jeronicus bent over his desk, and peered through rotating glass lenses. "Is someone talking to me?" He kept his head down. "No, it couldn't be somebody talking to me because the only person talking to me couldn't be talking to me because they're so busy doing their chores."

Journey stopped polishing. "But Grandpa, I don't want to—"

"Talking," he said tersely, but not unkindly.

"I was just trying to—"

"Chores," he cut in again.

Huffing, Journey turned and walked away, then stopped. Slowly she spun back around. While Jeronicus rotated a colorful green lens and squinted through it, Journey snuck back up behind him, spying on what he was starting to scrupulously write down. She'd recognize a mathematical notation anywhere. If she couldn't get him to like having her around, then at least she could learn from the greatest inventor of all.

But, as she watched over his shoulder and saw him finish the formula, she couldn't prevent herself from teaching *him*. "You have to raise the variable exponentially to the second power."

Jeronicus didn't look up, but he made the slight adjustment to the formula.

Journey chuckled. What was he thinking? Wasn't it obvious? "The other one," she shared.

"No, that's not possible." He scrutinized the formula. She was right. He made the change then turned to her with a mystified expression. "You understand this?" he asked incredulously.

She gave a sanguine nod.

"What about . . ." He reached across his note-cluttered desk and pulled out a piece of paper with another formula written on it in peculiar concentric circles. "This one?" he asked, testing her ability.

"That's the circumference of spectacular," she said with aplomb.

"And this?" He reached for another page marked with a sort of bell curve.

"The second derivative of sensational," she said proudly.

Jeronicus stared long and hard at her, baffled. "You've been looking through my notes," he accused. Only he and Jessica had ever been able to understand such things. And yet . . . He snatched up a blank sheet of paper and jotted down one more zany formula. She tried sneaking a peek over his shoulder, but he kept the note hidden. "Hey, hey! Watch it!" he warned as she wiggled this way and that. "Wait until I'm finished."

Finally, he stopped writing and turned to her. "You're not gonna trick me with this one. What about *this*?" He offered her the note. There was no way she'd deduce *that* theorem. He doubted anyone with a sound mind could understand it. If she could, then maybe, just maybe, she could help him with creating his something revolutionary in order to save his shop.

She contemplated it then looked up at him vacantly.

Jeronicus sighed, pursing his lips. "That's what I thought," he said sadly, turning back to tweaking away with a pair of rusty needle-nose pliers. "It's okay," he added gently.

"Well," she said, "it *would* be the square root of possible . . ."

Jeronicus froze. She *could* understand it! Because she wasn't just anyone with a sound mind; she was a Jangle, whose minds were unbelievable and full of soundness—and sounds!

"But there's a miscalculation," she stated. She stared off into space, and then, before Journey's eyes, neon-blue lines and symbols appeared in the air directly in front of her. She had unlocked this special, magical side of her long ago, after which Jessica had shared that Journey had inherited the ability from her grandfather. This was why it had been so important for Journey to meet Jeronicus. But while she'd operated her magic before, she had never seen it glimmer and dazzle so brilliantly, so vibrantly, so clear!

Refusing to let her excitement distract her, Journey focused in as she heard her imagination ignite. Noises echoed and clanged over one another, until they coalesced into one clear inner voice that showed her the way. Intuitively lifting her hand, she sifted through the glowing numbers and letters, and used her finger to write an even longer calculation in the air. The intervals and functions and decimals sparkled before her.

Jeronicus couldn't see the magic like he'd once been able to. Still, he watched. Still, he knew.

Journey finished writing the formula, and stopped to study it amid her utter exhilaration. There it was, shimmering before her like a starry galaxy full of answers. An accomplished smile cometed across her face. "Now it should work," she said with a certain, elated bob of her head.

Jeronicus stared at her in fascination. "You can see that?" he breathed. Not even Jessica had inherited his magical ability. It must have skipped a generation.

SISSON ARMS
JANGLES AND THINGS

Buy ONE
Buy ANOTHER
Bout of Generosity

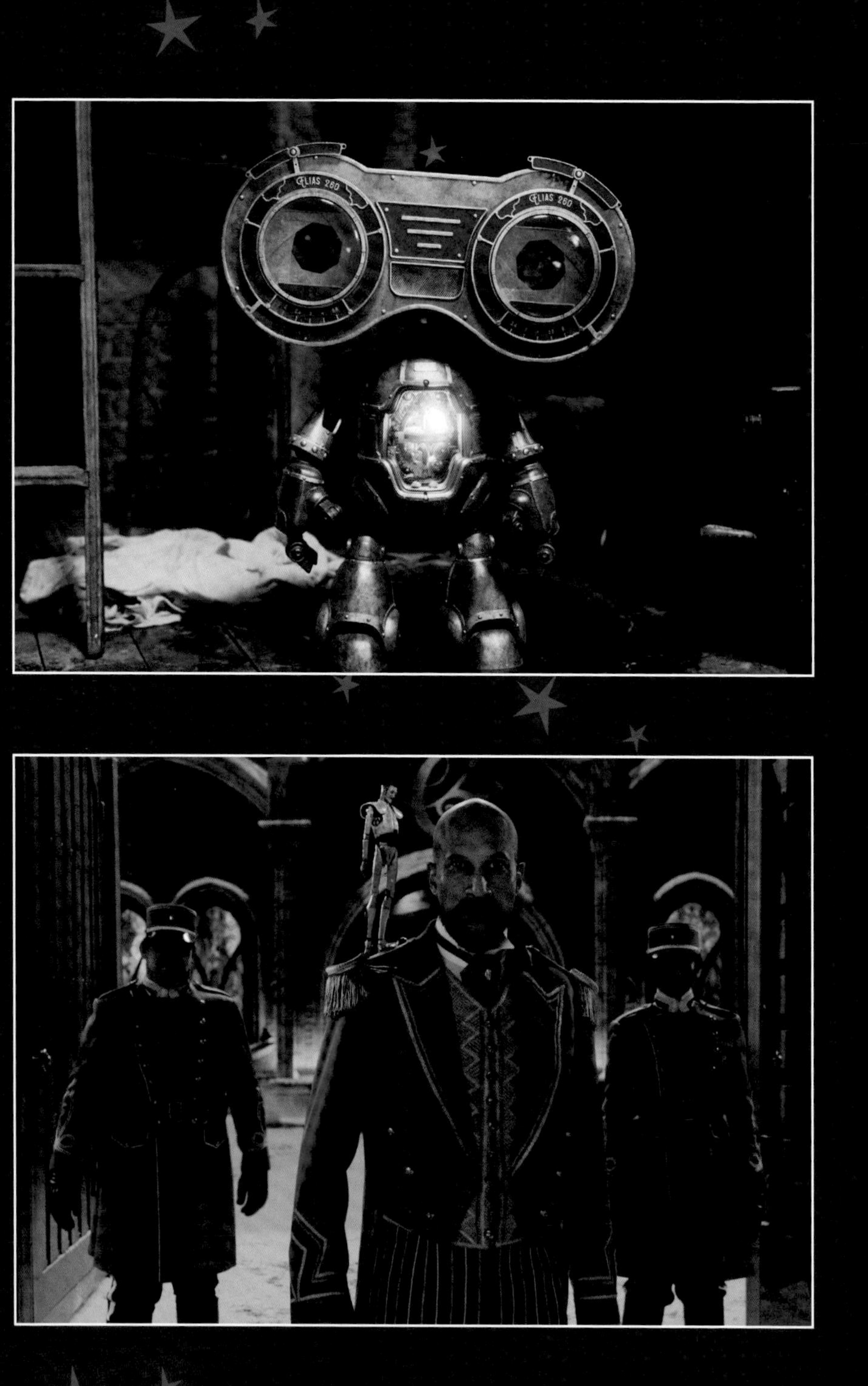
ELIAS 260
ELIAS 260

CRUSHER
Marvellous

She turned to him with an inquisitive smile. "Can't you?"

"No. Not anymore." At that, he stood and began to retreat down the hall.

Journey could see that she had accidentally touched a nerve. "I was just—"

"No more talking. Chores," he reminded her in a singsong, vanishing through the doorway and into the lonely darkness that lay beyond it.

Journey set her rag down on the desk and slumped her shoulders. Something must have happened to her grandfather to cause his magical ability to submerge in the murk of his mind, or, perhaps, of his heart.

Just then, something on the desk caught her eye . . .

A book open to a page of eccentric color-penciled doodles and designs. Picking it up, she regarded robot designs, then flipped the book and read the gilded name on the cover: **JESSICA J**.

Journey scrunched up her nose. "Mom?"

Meanwhile, Gustafson was baffled

by his broken, busted Werly Twerly . . .

Chapter Twelve

A mystified Gustafson scrutinized his own design for the Werly Twerly from his polished desk.

His entire office was opulent, with ornate wallpaper and rich pinewood paneling, a domed lamp with intricately cut pieces of colored glass, and oil portraits of Gustafson and Don Juan, all lit by candles, bulbous wall sconces, and sunlight through long stained glass windows. Gustafson feared that if he didn't get his act together, he'd end up having to relinquish it all.

"Well, maybe next time someone will lose an eye so they'll never have to see what a *mockery* you've become." Don Juan mounted a miniature staircase that led to the top of Gustafson's desk where Don Juan's own scaled-down office also lay, dwarfed by a large decorative gold egg.

Gustafson slammed down the page. "If you hadn't forced me to burn your designs, I could've mass-produced you," he said bitterly. He stood and wrestled off his jacket, flinging it to the floor in frustration. What was he to do about his quaking, crumbling, decaying dominion?

Don Juan chuckled nastily. "And the burden of building an empire would have fallen upon whom? I am, and forever will remain, one, and only one, of a kind." Don Juan strode gallantly across the desk toward his own minuscule one with its minute furniture and all.

Gustafson took the stopper out of a crystal decanter and poured himself a drink—cranberry juice, his favorite. "I *will* fix it. You'll see. Or I will come up with something even better!" he declared. "And you wanna know why? Because I'm the toy maker of the year! Toy maker of the year! Toy maker of the year! Toy maker of the year!" With each repetition, he pointed to the round **TOY MAKER OF THE YEAR** plaques hanging bountifully on either side of the door's archway.

"Lift me!" Don Juan commanded him.

Gustafson's face hardened in confusion.

"Do not be afraid," Don Juan urged. "I want to offer you sweet words of encouragement."

Gustafson picked up the pedestal on which Don Juan stood, like a pint-sized crow's nest one might find on a toy ship, so that they were eye to eye. And then Don Juan slapped him.

"I encourage *you* to not be an imbecile!" the matador yelled. "Your only successes have come from that book of inventions! So why not borrow another one of Jeronicus's inventions?"

Gustafson plunked him back down and stormed to the window. "Because I've already stolen—"

"Borrowed," Don Juan interceded.

"—everything in that book!" Gustafson continued. "There is nothing left of him! There is nothing left in that pawnshop of his!" He set down his cup and gazed into the darkening sky.

"Do you want me to slap you again? Because I'm happy to do it," Don Juan said. "Truly, once a great inventor, always a great inventor. There is *always* something left."

Slumped at the sill, Gustafson considered it. Could Jeronicus still have one last invention in him after all those years? Or perhaps a whole other book full of fresh ideas not yet explored?

"It's easy . . ." Don Juan reminded him, as he had once before, long ago.

Gustafson considered. With Christmas looming on the horizon, all that remained was supplying his factory workers with the blueprints for a new toy—one that actually functioned.

One that would again award him Toy Maker of the Year.

And he knew *just* where to get it . . .

Journey couldn't get over the notion that her mother may have been a great inventor, too . . .

Chapter Thirteen

Journey had taken her mother's book and sprawled out on a brocade sofa in a nook of windows.

Her own thoughts, like the light snow falling outside, began to drift. Poring over the pages, she grasped at the idea that her mother had also been an inventor, and she wondered why she'd never mentioned it. Her mother only ever told her of her grandfather's great mind, and how Journey had inherited his magical ability, but having seen him, she wondered what had happened to his shop, and to his spirit. She felt there was hope for her to do great things there. Miraculous things. Impossible things.

She studied the intricate robot design written in meticulous pencil lines, with its wide binocular-like eyes and hint of a mouth. She noticed a happy sketch of a cube, and recalled the mysterious glass one she had picked up, and how strangely protective her grandfather had been of it.

Then a new thought came . . . If her grandfather couldn't get his inventions to work, perhaps she could help! Journey was unstoppable.

With hope swelling in her chest, she shut the book, climbed on top of the front desk, and began to muster the magic inside her. The magic swirled around her and grew more concentrated in her open palms. All her life, she'd never felt like she fit in, but there, standing in the once-famous shop, Journey felt right at home. She released the splendid orbs of energy from her hands, and the magic projected around her, ensconcing her in a web of equations and numbers that lived in her head. Quotients and fractions. Decimals and coefficients. Calculations of additions and subtractions, brackets and parentheses. Her vision swam as she explored it all.

After she was done testing her ideas, the magic extinguished, and she glanced around the room, taking new details of it in. In the corner, a curious red, rounded fence adorned with metal florets caught her eye. Following a sudden sense of intuition—or maybe it was her magic—she made her way to it and stepped through its groaning little gate then pressed her boot down on a pedal. The platform began to rise up a pillar. It was an elevator. Before she knew it, she was headed straight toward the ceiling! But then, a hatch parted, and the elevator took her even farther up into a dark, wood-smelling abandoned room.

"Wow." She breathed, gazing around at her unexpected discovery.

She stepped off the elevator and it descended, vanishing behind her as she took in the large and drafty room. Despite the cobwebs coating flasks and beakers on the center table, the scuffed-up wooden floorboards, inventions covered in white gossamer sheets, and the stale air of neglect, Journey knew a creative space from any other kind of space, and this room buzzed with inspiring energy, even more than she'd first detected in the shop below. It vibrated through every molecule.

Passing an antique cabinet, she crossed to a covered invention and parted the sheet to get a gander. "Jangleator 2000?" she mused, disappearing under the sheet to marvel at the strange old machine.

"I *knew* it!" came a boy's awestruck voice. His tune quickly changed. "Ahh! A ghost!"

Journey emerged from behind the sheet as the boy cowered under a desk. Apparently, he had stumbled upon the elevator and had taken it up there—only to assume that the figure examining the Jangleator 2000 was a ghost. Striding toward him, Journey took in his green-and-orange tartan suit, green polka-dot bow tie, and owlish glasses with a makeshift magnifying lens clipped on.

"Who are you?" they asked each other in unison.

"I'm Journey," she said. "Jeronicus's granddaughter."

Edison stood to greet her. "I'm Edison. Edison Latimer.

Professor Jangle's *most trusted* assistant," he said with all the pride in the world.

Journey blinked at him, staving off an ounce of envy.

"You want to be my apprentice?" he asked optimistically.

"Do you want to be *mine*?" Journey asked him right back.

"I asked first," he said pointedly.

She sighed, shook her head, and walked away, eager to keep exploring.

"As the Head Inventor, I insist we leave at once," Edison called after her.

She combed over mysterious gadgets on the desk. "Not until I find what I'm looking for." She contemplated a cobweb-covered machine that resembled a typewriter, and kept searching.

"What are you looking for?" he inquired.

She opened the creaky little door of a dusty hutch. "I'll know it when I see it."

"You really shouldn't be touching anything in here because you never know when it could do something like—" He accidentally knocked over a kettle-like contraption that clattered loudly to the floor and rolled to a stop. Before it, there was an object covered by a ratty white sheet.

Journey crossed to it, with Edison chattering by her side. She tentatively pulled off the sheet to reveal a mechanical robot—the same one she'd seen in her mother's book of inventions! It was three feet of sturdy brass plates, with stocky arms and legs, and a head that practically resembled a pair of gigantic binoculars. The Buddy 3000.

Journey knelt to get a better look.

Edison followed suit. "There *is* something here. Why didn't the professor tell me?" He moved past his shock and dismay, and his face lit up. "It's— It's amazing!" he hollered.

Journey scoured the robot for an on switch, but couldn't find one. "It'll be even more amazing when *I* get it to work," she mumbled, deep in thought.

"If the professor couldn't get it to work, what makes you think *you* can?"

She looked at Edison, straightening her posture. "Because there's nothing that says I can't."

"What does that even mean?" Edison asked her.

She noted the robot had a square hole in the center of its chest, like it was missing a heart.

A *cube-like* heart . . .

"Wait." Her eyes widened. She had an idea.

After a quick stop downstairs, Journey returned to the workshop with the mysterious glass cube she'd noticed earlier. Carefully, she slid the cube into the cavity of the robot's chest with a gratifying *click*. She waited for it to turn on and activate. Nothing happened.

Edison knelt back down. "There's something wrong with it," he remarked.

"There'd be something wrong with you, too, if *you* were stuck in a dark room all your life," Journey retorted, her tone perhaps a bit more defensive than she'd intended. She found a page for the cube's design on the worktable while Edison peered over her shoulder. "It looks like the power source is in a superposition of states. We just need something to collapse the wave function."

They referenced the designs together. "So will it work or not?" he asked.

"Yes," Journey answered.

"What are you saying yes to?" Edison asked indignantly. "Will it work, or not? It's a simple question. All I request is a simple answer!"

"It will work," Journey said warmly. "At least I have to believe it will."

Just then, beeping and whirring sounded behind them. Journey and Edison whirled around, facing the robot, whose radial aperture-eyes were now open, whose glass cube now glowed and spun, and who had taken a few steps toward them. Journey and Edison turned back to each other.

And screamed.

Journey had found magic, and then some!

Good thing she had a new friend by her side.

Chapter Fourteen

"I don't want to die! I haven't even hit puberty!" Edison buried his face in Journey's back.

They'd hidden under the worktable together. "Edison! Let go!" Shaking him off, she inched out from under it. The robot, she saw, was just as scared as they were, peeping at her from around the table and mimicking her motions. "It's okay. Come on," she encouraged him.

The robot waddled toward her, wobbling as he grew accustomed to his newfound mobility.

"Easy," Journey told him.

The gears inside the robot's glass heart purred, and he steadied himself.

Journey motioned to herself. "My name is Journey."

Buddy regarded her, eyes dilating. *"Jeronicus's granddaughter."* He imitated what he'd heard her saying earlier!

"And this is Edison," Journey added, gesturing to the boy, who looked up.

He bonked his head on the bottom of the table. "Ow! I'm okay!" He crawled out from under it and tentatively clung to Journey's back. Finally, he gave a timid wave at Buddy. "Hi!"

"Why didn't you work for my grandfather?" Journey asked.

Buddy's eyes enlarged. *"It will work. At least I have to believe it will,"* he parroted back.

Journey gasped. "That's it." She rose. "Belief! It collapsed the wave function. It must've been part of the formula. He works because we believe," she told Edison, reviewing the page of the robot's designs.

"Well, *of course* we believe. He's hovering above your head," he said matter-of-factly. Sheer horror crossed his face as he realized what he'd said, and he reversed. "He's hovering above your head!" He ran and hid under the ladder of a stripped loft bed. "Mommy!"

Journey looked. Her jaw dropped, along with the page in her hands.

Buddy was levitating, somersaulting clumsily through the air. He knocked into wheels hanging from a wall, and then into ropes on a pulley system, as he tried to get his bearings.

Journey winced. "Be careful!"

Finally, after drifting helter-skelter, Buddy hovered evenly in place.

A whimsical wind blew through the workshop, and

Journey's cracked red boots lifted from the peeling floor. She began to rise high into the air. She was flying! She was actually flying! Buddy orbited around her like a satellite while Edison anxiously gazed up at them through the rungs of the ladder. Buddy swam expertly through the air, and Journey glided gracefully after.

Edison stepped out from under the loft bed, and the magic swept him off his feet. He grabbed hold of the ladder to prevent himself from floating, too, but his boots continued skyward. "What's happening?!" His fingers lost purchase then grasped on to the headboard.

"Edison, just let go! It'll be all right!" Journey vowed.

"It's not gonna be all right!" Edison's grip slipped. "Mom!" He grabbed a wooden beam jutting from the wall. Then he took a breath and let go, suspended in midair. He gawked then eyed his hands and body before starting to paddle his arms and kick his legs. Meanwhile, Journey and Buddy flitted around playfully, somersaulting and pirouetting with elegance.

What unexpected enjoyment they'd uncovered!

"Who's there in my workshop?!" came a voice.

Buddy instantly powered down and lowered shakily to the ground, going dark. His cube dislodged in the process, poking from his chest. Journey's boots alighted. Edison thumped face-first onto the bed, sending up a thick cloud of dust. The doors parted, and in stepped Jeronicus.

In his pajamas and threadbare dressing gown, he was

in no mood for hijinks. Consternation shone in his eyes at the sight of Buddy, fully assembled with his glass cube and all. "What are you doing up here?" He strode past Journey toward the robot. "What have you done?!"

Edison vaulted from the bed. "I told her not to touch it, but she's not a very good listener."

Jeronicus wheeled on her. "The contract clearly stated you were not to touch, move, bust, break, or take *anything* from this shop! Do you remember?" He took deep breaths.

"I-I didn't move it," Journey said, searching for the optimal words.

"You expect me to believe that it just got up and walked over here?" Jeronicus asked incredulously.

"Well, actually, he flew," Edison piped in from where he now stood at her side.

"That's not possible," Jeronicus scolded.

"It is, Grandpa J." Journey peeled Buddy's page of designs off the floor and handed it to her grandfather. "It works." While he perused it, she noticed doubt cloud her grandfather's features. He didn't believe them. In fact, she realized with a heavy heart, he didn't *believe* at all.

"Watch! I'll show you." Edison snapped the glass cube back into Buddy's chest.

Nothing happened.

Jeronicus gulped. "You see? You see? I *told* you. It doesn't work."

"It does," Journey implored. "You just have to *believe*!"

"Professor," Edison said, "you really are the greatest inventor of all!"

"I'm *not* an inventor," Jeronicus inserted. "And you're not an inventor, either."

Edison's brow furrowed, and he shot Journey a devastated glance. He'd never seen Jeronicus this upset. Crushed and quivering, he hung his head and scurried from the workshop.

Journey gaped at Jeronicus. "But Grandpa—"

"Enough already, okay?" he cut in despondently. "Enough. Nothing would make me happier than if this worked."

She woefully shook her head. "He does! You have to believe me! I'm telling you the truth! I would not lie to you, Grandpa. Please—"

"I need you to go to bed," Jeronicus butted in as he stalked with a shaky gait to the door.

"I don't *want* to go to bed. I want to stay up here and fix this. Please!" she pleaded. Her voice gave way to soft sobs. "Please, Grandpa! All you have to do is believe!"

"Will you listen to me?!" he growled, wheeling on her.

Journey was taken aback. Her lip trembled.

"Go!" he roared, gesturing sharply to the doorway. "Go!"

Shaking her head, eyes gleaming with hurt, Journey rushed past him.

Watching her flee reminded him of the only other time he'd watched someone he'd cared for leave. Only once her footfalls faded did Jeronicus realize he'd seen something in her that was reminiscent of what Joanne and Jessica also possessed. Another *J* word: joy. A fat tear rolled down his cheek as he thought about what his life might've been. He scanned his workshop, a place where his wife and daughter once cheered him on. He'd been stuck for so long. He wished he could somehow believe again. How he longed to rediscover that same magic within himself.

But, he concluded, it was too late for him.

He lifted a sheet, draped it over the lifeless robot, and retired to bed.

Journey realized that, like Buddy,

her grandfather was also missing a part.

Maybe she could fix that, too.

Chapter Fifteen

Gustafson had no trouble tracking down Journey that night, in spite of the late hour.

He could practically hear her sniffling from his factory. She sat dabbing her eyes on a stoop in a dark, chilly alley opening onto the empty square, Jeronicus's shop on the far side.

Better yet, she was alone.

His footsteps sounded along with the quiet taps of his bejeweled staff, which doubled as his cane, giving him away. "Hello, young lady," his smooth voice said from the shadows behind her.

Journey looked up from Gustafson's pair of shiny shoes and cloak to his top hat as he sat down. He leaned up his cane, removed his hat to reveal his bald noggin, and cleared his throat.

"Oh! Pardon my rudeness," he said. "I'm—"

"Gustafson," they said in unison. Journey knew who he was—the aspiring inventor in her mother's tales who stole from the Jangles in order to build his own toy factory and empire.

He grinned, taken aback. Then again, who *didn't* know his famous name? "Oh. Well done!" He gave a lighthearted chuckle. "And you must be . . . Jeronicus Jangle's granddaughter."

Journey stayed silent. In the same way she could see invisible formulas and missing parts, she could also tell when someone's heart was coated in a slimy, slippery layer of sleet.

"If I know anything about your grandfather, Jangles and Things is stirring with something sensational." He flashed an obsequious smile, hoping to get her to talk. "Something spectacular."

She could tell he was obviously fishing for information. It was almost as if somehow he *knew* about Buddy. "It's just a pawnshop," she stated unflappably with a shake of her head.

He leaned close. "You and I both know there's something in there. You can tell me. Perhaps I can market it or mass-produce it. For him." His insincerity was as clear as black ice.

Journey stared up from her boots at him. "I've got items to mark down." She leaned closer. "In the *pawnshop*," she added, for good measure, then stood. She was a tour de force.

Gustafson seized her by the wrist. She spun to him, frozen in fear, willing him to unhand her. Then, as quickly as he'd grabbed her, he let go. He smirked. He would find another way.

She took off across the square, the arctic chill of his bony fingers still lingering.

Sunrise welcomed the day before Christmas, marking the last chance for people to find the perfect present.

Chapter Sixteen

Cobbleton rang out with an excited cacophony of holiday-inspired sounds.

Honking cars and whinnying horses. Clanging bells and shouting vendors. Everyone tipping their hats to each other. Though not everyone was in the holiday spirit.

A sign had been taped to the door of Pawnbroker:

GOING OUT OF BUSINESS

BUY ONE, GET TWO FREE

(BUT ONLY IF YOU BUY THREE MORE!)

Inside, among stacks of moving crates, Edison fitted a lid over one. He had donned an orange coat and hat, rainbow trousers, a velvet waistcoat over a yellow shirt, and a coral-colored bow tie.

Journey appeared from upstairs, looking beautiful in a fitted leather jacket with a white faux-fur trim, royal-blue skirt, and yellow bow tie—though her expression looked anything but jolly.

"Did you hear? The professor's franchising!" Edison excitedly relayed to her as he continued to pack. Apparently, he thought Jeronicus was moving into a bigger and better store in order to sell his inventions—maybe even into a factory of his own.

"Edison, he's not franchising. He's closing the shop," she corrected him with a sad edge to her voice. "But not if *I* can help it!" She knew the shop was something special—and much, much more than just a pawnshop. Maybe she could convince Jeronicus that it was truly a magical place, too. Ducking, she took off in search of her grandfather.

It wasn't long before she found Jeronicus in the wintry square, and they walked side by side in silence. There was a frigidness in the air that had little to do with the inclement weather.

"Journey, I shouldn't have yelled at you," he said. "Now, please come along. I need to find Mrs. Johnston." They turned down a bustling side street lined with shops, each with lines out the door, and trolleys loaded with wares. Children frolicked past them through the crowds. Everything smelled like gingerbread and vanilla with the musk of pine and the scent of fresh snow.

"Happy holidays!" a pleasant voice cheered. It was undeniably Ms. Johnston.

Jeronicus handed Journey his basket full of packing supplies. Then he walked to Ms. Johnston, who helped the greengrocer carry a heap of parcels into her nice, warm establishment.

Ms. Johnston looked radiant in an ocean-blue dress, waistcoat, and jacket, her flat-brimmed hat bedecking her head. She approached the open back of a cherry-red mail truck, which boasted stacks of packages. When she noticed Jeronicus heading toward her, she froze up, thrilled.

"Mrs. Johnston!" he called out. "Mrs. Johnston! I've been looking for you all day. You always come by the shop. Is something wrong?" he asked. "Is everything all right?"

"Jerry. What a surprise!" She slowed her steps toward the back of the mail truck.

"What's the problem?" Jeronicus pressed. "Are you all right?"

She moved behind one of the truck's open doors and composed herself, then stepped out and ran her gloved fingers coolly along the edge of the door. "It's new. Do you like it?"

He regarded the mail truck. "Nice truck," he confessed.

"Isn't it?" She nervously yanked a cluster of mistletoe from inside, sticking it out over her hat. Glancing up at it, she feigned shock then tittered. "How did *that* get there?"

"Mrs. Johnston, I . . . I don't have time for this," he said with a little laugh and shake of his head. "I just need you to collect my boxes—"

"I know. I know!" She dropped the mistletoe back into the truck, deflated. "You have boxes that need collecting."

She picked up mail. "Everyone in Cobbleton has boxes that need collecting!" she said, dumping parcels and envelopes into his hands. "Only they've all gone for the holidays to be with their families. And *loved ones* . . ." she added longingly.

"Focus, Mrs. Johnston," he said gently. "Focus."

She snatched back his mail. "You know, Jerry, a little fun wouldn't kill you!" she snarled. Then she hurled the parcels and letters into the back of her truck. She went to slam the doors, but they jammed, so she irritably fussed to shut them until finally she managed to fumble the latch shut, nervous under Jeronicus's serene, watchful gaze. Maybe she'd overreacted a touch.

"Good job," he complimented her once she'd done it.

She brushed off her skirts and took a cleansing breath, wishing it'd be different. She yearned for him to see her for who she was. And, even more importantly, to see his brilliant self.

"Mrs. Johnston," he said, trying to get her attention as she moved around to the front of her truck. "Mrs. Johnston, I need this taken care of today."

"Happy holidays, Jerry." She sidled into the driver's seat.

"I'm closing the shop in a few days," he added solemnly.

"It's snowing!" she exclaimed with a hearty chuckle, in denial about the news. As he opened his mouth again to say more, she cut him off, maintaining her upbeat demeanor. "I hear your granddaughter's here." She slammed her hands on the steering wheel exaltedly. "Oh! Grandchildren are like children! Only you can give them back," she said.

"If you could just give me the time of day," Jeronicus tried again.

She laughed and kicked on the truck's engine, which sputtered.

Jeronicus reached in to help her.

She swatted his hand away. "It's fine, Jerry! I've got it!" She gripped the wheel with aplomb and straightened in her seat. It was clear she was still getting accustomed to her new vehicle.

He reached back in and released the emergency brake. "Here we go," he said.

"Thank you, Jerry!" she said.

"You'll come by, though. You'll come by, right?" He sounded desperate.

"Of course, Jerry!" She faced forward. "And off we go!" She honked her horn. "Get out the way!" she screamed to those strolling peacefully through the snowy lane.

Jeronicus called after her as the truck jostled away. "My name is Jeronicus!"

"It's Jerry!" she called back, followed by a few jolly honks of the horn.

Shaking his head, he spun around—only to get hit square in the face with a snowball!

"Hey!" He surveyed the busy street for his assailant.

Wham!

Another snowball hit him dead in the chest.

"Okay! Okay. Whoever that is, you're in for it," he challenged.

An old lady sipping tea in a window arched her brow with a tilt of her head toward the lane. He followed her quiet tip-off, and his sights landed on Journey peering out at him behind sacks of flour piled up on the street outside the bakery, hand full of fresh and sparkling snow.

"Journey?" he asked incredulously.

His granddaughter took a step out into the lane and chucked a snowball, which exploded against him upon impact. She let out a cheer and dodged back behind the tall stack of flour bags.

"You asked for it." Jeronicus strode to a shop window and began writing a formula into the frost on the pane with his finger. Children spied on him from inside another shop across the lane, watching him finish his equation, take snow from the sill, and pack it into his gloved hands.

Journey watched, too. Her eyes went wide. What did her grandfather have up his sleeve?

As if in answer, Jeronicus arched back his arm and let the snowball rip through the air. It sailed down the lane, with Journey and the other children watching it move as if by remote control, maneuvering past shoppers, vendors, and a horse until it vanished into the pale, distant sky.

Journey faced her grandfather, cackled gleefully, and waggled her fingers at him as if they were taunting moose antlers. "You missed me!" she teased, realizing it wasn't a fair match.

But then, the snowball came sailing back around like a boomerang and—

Wham!

Hit her right in the face!

She looked at Jeronicus, bewildered.

Jeronicus waggled his fingers back at her. "Oh! Somebody got hit with a snowball!" He beckoned for the onlooking children to join him. "I need some help," he said as they neared.

Journey nodded, impressed. So she had herself some fierce competition after all. She ducked back behind the flour bags and wrote out a formula in the air. Two could play at this game. As she kept devising a winning equation for the oncoming duel, she recruited two girls her age to join her in her efforts. "Hey, you want to come play with me? Give me some snowballs!"

The girls scrounged up snow, unable to see what Journey was seeing as she continued to write in the air. Jeronicus, however, could see the faint glow of her letters and symbols. A boy handed him a snowball. When he looked back up, he could no longer see the flicker of magic.

In moments, Journey's formula was complete, and the teams had been formed: girls with Journey and boys with Jeronicus. She let her snowball fly. Midair, it split into four snowballs, which hit Jeronicus and the three boys. Journey and her friends whooped and danced in triumph.

Jeronicus gaped. Then he and his team fired away. Their snowballs fell short. Still, he joined his teammates in a merry little dance, and gave them high fives as they circled him. He broke out into a smile, which seemed to be contagious. The old lady in the window laughed raucously, entertained by the old man's spirits. Then a giggle slipped from his mouth, as if on ice. More townspeople stopped to stare. They hadn't seen him laugh like this in many years.

The children continued to pack snowballs and let them soar. It was a snowball fight for the ages—pure, good, old-fashioned fun without any more formulas. A few passing townspeople got caught up in it, joining in. At one point, the whole lane partook in the lively, snowy reverie.

Journey emerged through the melee. "Grandpa J! This is so much fun!"

Jeronicus flung a snowball right at her, grinning mischievously.

But his snowball hit the constable instead, who'd stepped in the middle of the fight.

More snowballs hit him from every direction.

Jeronicus's expression fell as he watched the constable wipe snow from his face.

He locked eyes with Jeronicus, who held out his arms as if ready for the handcuffs.

After Journey smooth-talked their way out of the situation, they returned to Pawnbroker.

"Edison!" Jeronicus called as he set foot back in his shop, with Journey behind him. "Of course. He's probably out there somewhere having fun." He set down his giant basket. "Much packing to do. Much time to be made up." He gestured. "See to it that these boxes are full."

Journey indignantly tossed back her head. "But Grandpa, I don't want to be—"

"Packing," he reminded her, striding ahead.

"Grandpa, I was just trying—!"

"Boxes!" He marched upstairs. "Try to find the synchronicity between the two."

Journey stuck out her lip. He really needed to lighten up. And where was Edison? Her grandfather was probably right and Edison was off having fun, maybe even having a snowball fight of his own. She picked one of the flyers up from off an old trunk whose bold letters shared that Pawnbroker was going out of business. She sighed. Then something on the floor caught her eye . . .

Edison's glasses.

She picked them up and studied them. How odd.

Thud! Thud! Thud!

There was a loud banging from upstairs.

She rushed up to the workshop to find Edison, tied with a thick rope to the leg of the worktable. She rushed over. "What happened?!" Her nimble fingers hastened to free him.

"Gustafson!" Edison cried. "He started bragging that he was the greatest inventor, and how the professor hadn't invented anything in years, and—"

Journey pulled the rope off him, and stared. "Edison, tell me you didn't."

He frowned. "I'm the worst apprentice ever. I mean, you're a really bad apprentice, but not even close to how bad I am!"

Journey looked around. Just as she'd feared, the robot was gone. "Buddy," she breathed.

Edison went to stand and bumped his head on the bottom of the table. "Ow! I'm okay." Rubbing his noggin, he stood to join her.

"Where's Buddy?" she asked frantically.

"I think I hear my mother calling me! Did you hear that? I definitely did." Edison charged for the door. "Here I come!"

"Edison," Journey said unyieldingly.

He paused in the doorway and glanced sheepishly back at her.

She took a heartened breath. "We *have* to get Buddy back."

Much to Journey's surprise, Edison nodded resolutely. "Yes, we absolutely do."

Minutes later, Journey and Edison raced through the town and stopped in an alcove when they spotted Ms. Johnston's mail truck parked on a sloping street. They quietly peeked out at it.

"Are you thinking what I'm thinking?" Journey asked.

Edison gulped. "If I say no, will you stop thinking it?"

Journey quirked an eyebrow. Then she bolted toward the truck, with Edison reluctantly following. They climbed into the open back, past piles of packages tied with string and stacks of sealed letters—likely presents and cards that might barely make it to their recipients before the big day. Just as they vanished into the depths of the truck, Ms. Johnston emerged from the florist's.

"It's new! I'm still getting used to it," she called merrily to the florist. "I only almost killed *one* person today!" she joked. "Progress!" Then she closed the back of her truck, unwittingly sealing Journey and Edison in complete and utter darkness.

While most children their age were settling in for Christmas Eve, Journey and Edison sat in the cardboard-scented gloom as the truck lurched forward and started to Gustafson's Factory.

Journey would stop at nothing to rescue Buddy.

It was her only hope of saving the shop, and the fate of her grandfather as well.

THAT VERY SAME CHRISTMAS EVE,

GUSTAFSON HAD FOUND ANOTHER WAY

TO PUT HIS WICKED PLAN INTO PLAY . . .

Chapter Seventeen

Gustafson admired his reflection in the mirror and adjusted his purple sash.

"The buyers are here? Again?!" Don Juan spoke to Gustafson from where he stood on his raised pedestal. "Did you not learn your lesson the last time?"

Gustafson straightened his neckerchief. "We saw it with our very own eyes." He referred to when he and Don Juan had used their spyglass viewers (one human-sized and one doll-sized) at the office window to watch on the two children flying in Jeronicus's workshop with the Buddy 3000. There was always something left indeed. And Gustafson had found it. It was why he'd gone out sniffing for information, though Journey had been reticent to divulge any. The fearful boy, however, had been more willing, or perhaps merely easier to trick. As soon as Gustafson had set his tall green music box down in the shop while the boy was packing, Edison was practically hypnotized by it. Stealing the robot after coercing the boy into telling him where it was had been simple. Tying the boy up, less so. But he had what he needed, and then some. Just like old times. A Jeronicus Original . . .

He strode to Don Juan and chuckled. "It's foolproof!"

Don Juan slapped Gustafson across the cheek.

Gustafson recoiled, warily touched his own face, and winced.

"You are proof that there are fools! Fools, fools, fools, fools, fools!" Don Juan chided.

Steeling himself, Gustafson left to go meet his buyers. While every person had wanted the perfect gift for Christmas Day, Gustafson had been desperate and determined to deliver it.

They were going to love their shiny new toy.

And *this* time, it would work.

Journey knew Gustafson would go

to any lengths to figure out how Buddy worked.

She had to keep the last spark of hope alive,

not only for her grandfather and his shop,

but also for herself . . .

Chapter Eighteen

The mail truck crossed over the spindly suspension bridge that divided the town in half, heading toward Gustafson's Factory, spewing acrid black smoke and glowing with sickly green lights.

Ms. Johnston pulled up and hopped out with her mailbag. Journey and Edison peeked out, eyes sweeping the grounds. Guards patrolled the entrance, stationed outside the high wall.

Then they raced through a maze of walls, rounded a corner, and stopped in their tracks.

Up ahead, they faced a giant, propeller-like fan with huge steel blades set into a grate. The big blades were motionless, so that beyond them, Journey and Edison could see a circular tunnel of sorts . . . an air duct leading back into darkness . . . A way into the factory!

Edison shivered. "We can't go through there."

"Whether you think you can or think you can't, you're right," she said, running headlong between two of the huge stationary blades and safely into the dark, green-tiled air duct.

"What does that even mean?" he called out behind her.

But she kept running, so he had no choice but to chase after her.

They moved through the tunnels until, eventually, they pushed up a little metal grate, and stepped out of the duct through the opening and into a packing room full of wooden crates and an oil lantern. Journey could tell that it led into a hallway beyond.

A voice sounded from somewhere in the factory. "I now present to you the premier pioneer of playtime products, and twenty-eight-time toy maker of the year! A man whose artistic excellence is unparalleled! Whose technological prowess is unmatched!"

At that, Journey tugged Edison's sleeve. "Come on! Come on!" She led him around a dark bend. They rushed down the rest of the hallway until they reached a slightly open door. They peeked through the crack and into a room, where a man was addressing a small, seated crowd.

"The marvelous, miraculous, master of magnificence . . . The greatest inventor in *all* the land . . . Gustafson!"

The announcement was followed by a smattering of applause.

"Thank you." A far set of double doors opened, and

Gustafson, in his suit, sash, shoulder cape, and tall top hat, spun around and stepped out onto a dais. "An interactive robot!" He flashed a dazzling grin, giving the same sort of pomp and circumstance from his days as a young apprentice. "What child could resist?" he inquired dramatically with a smug look on his face.

Journey and Edison moved around to the back of the showroom to get a better look, peering through the set of open double doors and down past the dais as Gustafson took the floor.

"My latest! My greatest!" He rested his hand over what Journey and Edison knew to be the robot covered by a satin sheet, pausing for dramatic effect. "The Buddy 3000!"

The sheet came away with a whisper. There, under a spotlight for the buyers to see, standing on a little table, was Buddy, his brass plates glowing golden in the light.

Gustafson tossed the silk sheet to his Head of Production, who caught it with ease. Then he pushed the cube fully into Buddy's chest with a rewarding *click*.

Nothing happened.

Gustafson lifted his chin high. "We are simply waiting for it to warm up," he assured.

Buyers exchanged glances, not wholly convinced.

"I was working on the housing and, um . . ." His fingernail rapped the cube. "Hello?"

A few contentious buyers snickered while others attempted to stifle their mocking laughter. Some skeptically quirked their brows. One woman stood, chortling, and began to waltz out.

"Oh no! Don't miss it!" Gustafson warned her. "Cause you don't wanna miss it." He rested a hand on Buddy. "This is going to be amazing. The wow factor alone will knock your socks off," he promised. Though he felt just as he had in his crummy youth: like a dud.

Buyers began to raucously laugh.

Sweat beaded on Gustafson's brow. He rambled, hands tightly clasped. "I've used tin cogs as opposed to copper cogs and it makes the product lighter, which is easier for transportation when you bring it into your home for your children during this holiday season! Twenty-eight-time toy maker of the year!"

"They don't believe!" Journey and Edison whispered to each other.

For although the greatest inventions in the land had been stolen by Gustafson, the title of the greatest inventor in the land was not something that could be taken. Especially when Gustafson's inventions no longer worked, sputtering out like lost dreams—and he hadn't expected for Jeronicus's robot to backfire.

Journey knew that like an exacting formula, karma always netted out to zero in the end.

The showroom began to empty out, with buyers giggling their way through the open doors leading out into the crisp night, until the only one left was Gustafson's Head of

Production, who stood stoically on the other side of Buddy. The doors slammed shut, sending a cold draft gripping the back of Gustafson's neck.

The sheen of showmanship slipped from Gustafson's put-on cheerfulness. "Box this wretched thing up and send it where we send all ill-conceived toys," Gustafson commanded, marching back toward the dais, where Journey and Edison were still spying through the doors.

"To retail, sir?" the Head of Production clarified.

"No!" Gustafson roared. "To the Crusher!"

The Head of Production gaped. "The Crusher?"

"Yes! The Crusher!"

Journey and Edison looked at each other, eyes wide.

This wasn't good. They had to save Buddy!

They scrambled up and booked it down the hall.

A short while later, Journey and Edison gazed through the rails of a balcony at two guards on the floor below. They pushed a crate containing Buddy toward a noisy machine that looked like a glowing steel furnace. It made an awful racket, and steam hissed from its vents. The Crusher!

"I'll distract them and you go get the crate." Journey popped up above the railing and waved. "Hey!"

The guards looked up and saw her, then she took off down the hallway and they gave chase from below. Meanwhile, Edison sneaked down the stairs by the Crusher.

He stealthily approached the crate, stopping short behind a pillar to make sure the coast was clear. The crate rested on top of a moving dolly—a wide wooden base with swivel wheels, a long metal handle, and a length of rope coiled up under the wheels. The crate itself had large slots in the wooden lid, and Buddy stared up lifelessly from inside. Edison took the handle of the moving dolly, and pulled.

He wheeled the crate around in a semicircle across the stone floor before gliding it down a smog-choked hall lit by dim bulbs hanging from the ceiling. Just then, two more uniformed guards clomped up a set of stairs from below. Edison kept going. The faster he ran, the faster the wheels of the dolly spun, clacking over metal scaffoldings. He burst into a warehouse room and rushed across a platform next to an oscillating machine, crate bumping along from behind.

Journey flew up a set of side steps and nearly smacked into him.

"The guards! They're right behind me!" he cried, not slowing down.

Journey pushed the crate, joining him. "Come on! We have to get back to the tunnel!" She realized she wanted to commend him for his bravery. "You're doing great, Edison!"

"You're lying!" he shot back.

An alarm blared. Red lights flashed. Guards swarmed the halls.

Journey and Edison passed into the packing room and secured the giant doors, taking care to bolt the locks. Then they were running the crate back across the room toward the open grate.

"Edison! We have to hurry!"

They moved past piled crates, jolting one, which sent a ladder knocking over the oil lantern. It fell into an open crate full of hay. The flames danced ominously in the glass globe. But Journey and Edison were too focused on their escaping to have noticed.

"Intruder alert! Unauthorized children have been spotted on the premises! Apprehend them at once!" said a voice on an intercom.

They pushed the crate through the opening and stepped into the circular tunnel to join it.

Edison yanked the handle in an effort to rotate the dolly, but the handle broke in his grip! "Oh no! It snapped off!"

Whoosh! Whoosh! Whoosh!

Suddenly, there came a whirring from below. The sound of spinning blades.

Journey and Edison turned to one another. "Is that the fan?" Edison cried.

It had been scary enough to pass the blades when they had been still.

Now the blades were whirring like wild.

What could Journey and Edison do?

Jeronicus wandered up to his workshop,

where he had found neither kids nor robot . . .

Christmas Eve was beginning to lose its shine.

Chapter Nineteen

Jeronicus looked around the dark and noisy square, alive with Christmas Eve celebrations.

"Excuse me, sir! Sir? Have you seen my granddaughter?" he asked the butcher. "Her name's Journey. She's about this tall." He moved his arms to demonstrate her height.

The butcher shook his head.

"She has cogs and screws in her hair!" Journey told the greengrocer.

The greengrocer gave a shrug.

"She's precocious! Annoyingly smart. But you like her once you get to know her! I'm getting there! I'm getting there!" he called to the carriage driver, whose eyes darted sideways.

Jeronicus's face fell. No one had seen Journey or Edison. His concern grew grave. Where had they gone? He moved to search a different part of the lane when his sights fell on a posted flyer.

GUSTAFSON: MASTER OF MAGIC

-PRESENTS-

THE BUDDY 3000

TONIGHT ONLY!

He stared. It couldn't be. They couldn't have forked over his things . . .

Just then, he spotted Ms. Johnston driving her truck down the icy lane.

"Mrs. Johnston! Mrs. Johnston!" He stepped in front of the now-idling vehicle.

"Jerry!" she called out the window, delighted. "Jerry!"

"Could you take me to Gustafson's factory?"

"Oh, Jerry, of course! Hop inside," she called cordially.

"*Jeronicus.* My name is *Jeronicus.*" Still, he climbed in beside her.

"When you're walking, it's Jeronicus. When you're riding with me, it's Jerry!" she said in an affectionate singsong. Then she clutched the wheel, and the truck lurched forward. Cars and trucks were still fairly new to the world, and she was still fairly new to driving one, which may have showed.

The slippery, sliding trek sent Jeronicus's stomach into knots, until eventually the truck grumbled across the endless bridge and jerked to a stop before the factory's armed front gates.

Jeronicus crept out the side of the truck and tiptoed around to the back.

"Me again!" Ms. Johnston called to a guard.

"What business have you now?" the approaching guard quizzed her.

"Well, you see," Ms. Johnston began, "I-I forgot to deliver these, didn't I? Oh! Silly me! You know what it's like, it being Christmas Eve and everything with all these parcels and gifts, you name it!" She eyed the label of a package in her hands and flipped it over before giving it very slowly to the guard.

Meanwhile, Jeronicus secretly made his way toward the side of the factory. He followed a high brick wall that zigged this way and zagged that, a sort of snowy maze with pillars topped with green lanterns, until he turned a corner and faced a wall of monstrous blades leading to a tunnel beyond. He almost set foot inside when the motionless blades began to spin like a giant airplane propeller, blowing him back in a brisk and intense gust of wind—and barring him from entry.

What could Jeronicus do?

The robot hadn't worked like Gustafson had hoped, and he had no Plan B. At least not yet . . .

Luckily, there were still a few hours left before Christmas morning was upon him.

Chapter Twenty

Don Juan admired his reflection in a miniature paneled mirror.

He turned to view every angle of his perfect design. "Your hair, as shiny as a stallion's mane. Your eyes, the azul of the sea. And your buttocks like the burn of a fresh jalapeño that's just about to pop—"

"Do *not* finish that sentence please!" Gustafson reared up from his seat and loomed over the toy matador, hands splayed on his glossy desktop.

At that moment, guards in green uniforms studded with gold buttons marched into the office and stood at rapt attention.

"There are kids in the factory," one said. "They've taken the crate with the robot."

"Who cares!" Gustafson growled as he sank down in his chair and threw his arms out. "It's a failed invention! Let them have it."

"¡Ay! ¡Dios mío! If it were *failed*, then why would they be trying to recover it?" Don Juan said. "They wouldn't!"

Gustafson's pout gave way to wide-eyed comprehension.

Maestro Don Juan Diego was rarely wrong.

"Stop them at once!" Gustafson ordered.

Journey's heart was as brave as it was pure.

It was how she knew that, together,

friends could overcome anything.

Chapter Twenty-One

"Is that the fan?" Edison's words echoed all the way down the chute to the gusty exit below.

"Edison?" a voice carried back up the tunnel to them.

Edison beamed his megawatt smile. "Professor!"

"Grandpa J!" Journey shouted over the loud droning of the fan.

"Journey? Are you all right?" Jeronicus's question rang in their ears.

"Yes!" Journey answered.

"No!" Edison said at the same exact time.

They looked at each other.

"Yes!" Journey yelled at Edison.

"No!" Edison shouted over her.

Journey jogged a few feet forward and stopped at the precipice where the tunnel's chute opened into the darkness below. "We're fine!" Journey called down to her grandfather.

"We've got Buddy! We just have to get him out of here!"

"Okay, I want you to turn back around right now! Right now! At once!" Jeronicus said. "I'll meet you at the gate!" The blades were deadly. They had to find a way out through the packing room.

Journey and Edison rushed back toward the crate, and halted when they noticed an eerie orange glow coming from inside the packing room. They stared at it through the grate.

Enormous flames were eating away at the crates and barrels inside!

The packing room had become a sparking and volatile inferno!

Edison stared alongside Journey in terror. "Fire!"

They raced back down the tunnel and stopped, calling into the chute.

"Grandpa J! There's a fire! We *have* to go through the blades!"

"Journey, listen to me!" Jeronicus's voice boomed. "You *cannot* go through the blades! It's impossible! That's impossible!"

Journey spun to Edison, eyes sparkling. "That's it. The square root of possible." She shouted back to Jeronicus: "That's it! The square root of possible!"

"It's just a theory!" Jeronicus hollered. "A formula in my mind! It's not been tested!"

"We trust you!" Journey yelled.

Edison cupped his hands and shouted, "We don't have a choice!"

"It's a *theory*!" Jeronicus bellowed.

But Journey trusted in her grandfather's theory more than anything. All her life, her mother had told her about how she and Jeronicus shared the same ability. His magic, she surmised, had been dormant for many years, but she could tell it was still there inside him. He just had to bring it back to life somehow!

The intercom voice reverberated in the tunnel. "We've tracked the intruders to a fire in the East Tower! All guards report to the fire in the East Tower!" Before Journey and Edison knew it, they could hear the guards battering the bolted doors in the packing supplies room, trying to burst inside.

Outside, Jeronicus didn't know what to do.

"Grandpa J, just believe!" he heard Journey cry.

Jeronicus rubbed his hands together and took a breath, then took great care to blow on each palm. He began to write in the sky with his finger, like old times. Nothing happened.

But then, the faintest light flickered.

He could barely see it, but it was there, just visible enough to see.

"Okay. Okay." Jeronicus mustered up more of that spirit. Swiftly, he wrote out additional ratios and intervals and fractions, shifting variables around with a practiced ease.

"Square root of possible. Velocity. Centrifugal force. Point of inertia," he mumbled, speaking the formula that had begun flowing through him. The mathematical notations blazed just as brightly as ever.

"Grandpa J!" Journey shouted down. "Hurry!"

Jeronicus tweaked the luminous formula, moving the last symbol into place so that the calculation made crystal-clear sense to him. "The blades are moving at five hundred revolutions per hectosecond!" he shouted into the tunnel. "You'll have to get caught in the current of the blades, which will sync with the speed of the crate and the path of inertia! You have to enter at a thirty-five-degree angle, at exactly fifteen hundred feet per minute! You will make it through!"

"Okay, Grandpa J!" Journey called out. "I love you!"

And then, as if by a Christmas Eve miracle, she heard the same words echoed back, but this time it wasn't just an echo. "I love you too, Journey!" Then he added: "It *is* possible!"

In the tunnel, she smiled then ran to the crate. "Let's go!" she said, trying to turn it.

Studying it, Edison had an idea. He pulled the rope out from the bottom of the dolly.

Journey shook her head at him, puzzled. "Edison!" What in the world was he doing?! "We don't have time for this! There's a fire!" She could hear the guards kicking down the doors of the fiery packing room, which sent out a burst of heat into the tunnel as something in the room exploded. Edison screamed as the flames reached out into the tunnel like serpents.

"We have to go!" Quickly, Journey pushed the crate as Edison harnessed the rope around the front of the box to create a steering wheel of sorts. He grabbed the front of the crate, and with Journey pushing it from the rear, they moved it toward the chute together.

Edison hopped on first, with Journey leaping up onto it behind him.

"Just for the record, this is *not* a good idea!" he yelled, sitting like a sleigh driver gripping the reins. The crate pitched down the tunnel, drifting side to side as they screamed, the wheels of the dolly underneath swiveling wildly.

Then the crate plummeted down the chute just as a fireball erupted after them.

Edison steered it this way and that down the slanted incline, the fireball hot on their tail.

"This is so cool!" Journey shouted gleefully, as if they were on a jolly sleigh ride.

"This is not cool!" Edison shrieked as the crate did a three-hundred-and-sixty-degree loop. "This is dangerous!"

Journey saw that they were heading toward support beams. "Duck!"

They leaned forward and pressed against the crate, narrowly avoiding the beams.

Edison glanced back at Journey. "That was close—"

"Edison, watch out!" She pointed ahead at a steaming pipe.

Edison jerked the rope, sending the crate swerving sideways to circumvent it.

Looking over their shoulders, they could see the flaming fireball was gaining.

"It's getting close!" Edison screamed. "This is crazy!"

"Edison, you just have to believe!" Journey shouted.

He nodded. "There's no logical reason that I should, but I do. I do!"

The wheels of the careening dolly began to screech.

"You have to slow us down!" Journey told him.

"We can't slow down!" he replied.

"Buddy!" Journey shouted, hoping—no, *believing*—he could wake to help them.

Just then, the crate glowed with a warm light.

In the next instant, Buddy's metal arms broke through either side of it, elongating and extending out to drag against the chute's tiles, slowing them down in a shower of sparks.

"How is he doing that?!" Edison remarked in a mixture of joy and fear.

The chute leveled out. They could see the blur of blades ahead, whipping louder and louder. There was no turning back. They saw Jeronicus standing beyond the blades, arms up.

"You're going too fast! Thirty-five degrees!" he warned.

Journey believed that Buddy would know exactly what to do.

The robot used his arms to strenuously launch them into the air.

Leaning back and flattening out, Journey and Edison screamed as the crate sailed in a perfect thirty-five-degree angle toward the big spinning blades, the white-hot flames licking at their necks . . .

They kept screaming and clinging to the crate for dear life.

And then, like magic, they were safely through.

Journey and Edison had believed in the impossible.

And for the first time in a long time,

so had Jeronicus.

Chapter Twenty-Two

The crate arced through the air, landed in the snow, and skidded to a stop.

Edison was knocked forward and fell facedown in the snow with a grunt. At the same time, the jet of fire erupted out of the tunnel and through the fan as Jeronicus dove to the side.

Journey dismounted the crate and ran to her friend. "Are you all right, Edison?"

He held out a thumbs-up. "I'm okay!" he groaned, starting to rise.

Just then, Jeronicus hobbled over. "Journey! Journey!"

She beamed and ran to him. "Grandpa J!" She hugged him, and he hugged her back. "Grandpa J, your formula," Journey said, not letting him go from their embrace. "It worked."

Edison dusted himself off and came running over.

"Professor!" He stopped short. "I came up with a steering mechanism made up of rope that got us through the tunnel alive," he said, sounding proud—and a bit winded.

"Well done, Edison," Jeronicus told him. "Quite the inventor!" They were words that Jeronicus may not have been capable of uttering when he'd had a different apprentice under his tutelage. They were also the words that Edison had been waiting to hear his whole short life.

Edison's eyes shimmered and he joined their hug. "Just like you," he said softly.

Ms. Johnston rushed out from around the corner and stopped at the sight of them.

Jeronicus gawked. "Mrs. Johnston?"

"A good postal woman always ensures a safe delivery." She reached out her arms. "Children! Jerry! Come on!" She started to run, then spun back to them. "I'll get the truck! You get the crate!" she assigned.

Jeronicus, Journey, and Edison happily followed her around the corner.

Within minutes, the mail truck rumbled off, slipping and sliding its way across the snowy suspension bridge. Was that Journey's very active imagination, or had she gazed out the window in the back of the truck to spy a tall figure stepping out from the factory's main gate into the night?

Soon, the truck was careening down Chancer Street, with Jeronicus shouting for townspeople taking late-night Christmas Eve strolls to get out of the way, headlights illuminating their shocked faces, until it buckled to a jarring stop in front of Pawnbroker. Jeronicus hopped out and ran around to the back of the truck, opening the doors to discharge Journey and Edison. Then he and Ms. Johnston heaved the crate from the truck. Journey held the shop door open as they carried it inside, and she followed in after them with Edison on her heels.

"Edison!" a voice called from down the shadowy lane as his foot touched the stoop. "Time to come home! It's getting late!"

He froze, slouched, and turned from the shop. It wasn't that he didn't want to spend the last shred of Christmas Eve with his mother, but that a small part of him wanted to spend it with the Jangles more—especially because he wanted to watch Jeronicus see Buddy powered up and in action for the first time.

"Edison, come on!" Journey emerged back on the stoop. "We're about to put Buddy together."

He strode to her, jabbing his thumb behind him. "My mom's calling me, so I've gotta go."

"Thanks for helping me rescue Buddy. I couldn't have done it without you."

He took a breath. "We both know that's not the case, but thanks for saying it anyway."

They shared a smile.

And then he took off as Journey gave a wistful little sigh and reentered the shop.

"Journey, I really, really do like you!" Edison called back. "A lot. Bye!"

At the sound of his confession, she ran back outside and watched him jogging down the lane, vanishing around a bend, where he crashed into something and shouted out in pain.

"Ow! I'm okay!"

Journey laughed and shook her head. Classic Edison. She was glad they were friends, and that he'd found his inner fearlessness. She'd known he'd had it in him. He just needed a push.

Jeronicus and Ms. Johnston stepped outside to join her.

"Grandpa, now you won't have to close the shop!" She darted past him inside.

Jeronicus was finally alone with Ms. Johnston. "Thank you," he told her. "Though I don't know why you came back." He followed her to her mail truck.

She turned to face him. "Because you're a good man," she said. "Stubborn. Ornery." She chuckled and slid into the front seat. "Could benefit from a good haircut, a new set of clothes, but . . . still good." She smiled out the window at him. Then she looked down at her hands on the steering wheel. "Jeronicus . . . I know about losing things. But the magic isn't *just* in what you've lost. It's in what you still have."

For a great thinker, he'd never thought of it that way before.

She revved her truck's engine to go.

"Mrs. Johnston." He corrected himself. "*Ms.* Ms. Johnston." He looked into the truck. "Oh," he said delighted. "Look what I found here." He pulled out her clump of mistletoe. "I forget how you use these," he added with a nervous glance.

They both regarded it for a long moment.

"It's been so long." He lifted it over her hat. "I think you place it over someone's head, like so," he said softly, "and *lean* in for a kiss."

Ms. Johnston looked to him and she chuckled, closing her eyes and leaning in.

Then he tilted through the window and pecked her on the cheek. "Like so."

She kept her eyes shut, savoring the moment.

"Ms. Johnston?" he asked. "Ms. Johnston? Can you hear me?"

After several seconds, her face broke into a grin.

"I'll— I'll keep the mistletoe," he said quietly once she'd zoomed away in a dreamy haze.

Jeronicus stepped back into the shop and watched Journey open the crate.

The Buddy 3000 poured from it in pieces. Metal plates. Screws. Gears. And cogs.

Apparently, the strain on the robot to decelerate Journey and Edison in the chute and to get them perfectly angled through the blades had been more than his tiny body could bear.

Journey fumbled with the bits of metal, her face falling, desperately trying to solve how to put them back together. She spied the robot's glass heart among the scrap pile and carefully lifted it.

"Grandpa, you have to fix Buddy," she urged Jeronicus. "You have to make him work again. Please." She handed the cube to him. She knew he could do it.

Wordlessly, he sat at the counter and turned it over.

Minuscule cogs poured onto the table.

"I can't."

"Yes, you can," Journey protested. "You're the greatest inventor of all! You can do anything! It's why I came here. I had to see it for myself."

"You're here because your mother wanted you here. It's what she wrote in her letter."

"Because I wrote her one from you saying the same thing."

Jeronicus craned his head up at her. "Why would you do such a thing?"

"All she ever talked about was how *magical* this place

was, and that you could see things that nobody else could!" Journey blinked earnestly. "Like I can."

He studied her. So, she fabricated the letter just to facilitate meeting him.

"Everywhere I've ever been, I've felt out of place. This is the only place where I finally felt like I belong." She looked at her cracked red boots, hanging her head.

Jeronicus tilted her chin to look up at him. He was glad she'd found her way to him in the end, no matter the means, and that she'd helped him find his way back to himself. "Journey, a child with imagination always belongs. Never be afraid when people can't see what you see. Only be afraid if you no longer see it. Okay?"

She nodded solemnly, and they shared a heartfelt embrace. "I love you, Grandpa J."

Long after Journey had gone to bed, Jeronicus carried the Buddy 3000 into his dimly lit workshop and carefully placed the robot's broken little body onto his worktable. It was time to get to the repairs, and to show his granddaughter when she woke up on Christmas the next morning the full extent of who her grandfather could truly be. He hunched over the table, clicked on his lamp, and polished Buddy's metal plates. He selected tools from his old smock then shrugged into it. It still fit.

He started on the fiddly work: the cleaning of washers and bearings, dials and pins. Then he moved on. He seamlessly welded metal mechanisms. Tightened screws. Banged his hammer.

At last, he blotted his brow with a kerchief and assessed his progress.

Not so far away in a cozy little cottage,

Jessica had made up her mind on a whim.

She would pay Cobbleton an early visit.

Chapter Twenty-Three

Back at Nesbitt Cottage, Jessica folded the letter from Jeronicus in the dark of her bedroom.

It was Christmas Eve, and she felt unexplainably compelled to pay him an early visit, to see if maybe, just maybe, he'd changed. She caught her travel cloak and feathered hat in the mirror of her boudoir, and exhaled, then made her way to her front door, where she cut the lights, enveloping her cottage in darkness. She stepped out into the chill night air, suitcase clutched shakily in her gloved hand.

Moments later, she sat back in the omnibus that was jostling over the snowy countryside, and she re-read Jeronicus's letter. It stated that he hoped they could make it work again, even if it wouldn't be easy. Her father had never really seen her after her mother died. He'd shut her out for good, consumed with his inventions and with trying to keep his reputation as the greatest inventor from slipping through his fingers like snow, as she faded away. Staring out the window, she hoped this time would be different. Suitcase in hand, she exited the omnibus into Cobbleton.

Shopkeepers closed their doors and drew their blinds. Patrons left the Sisson Arms pub. Men loaded up wagons with heavy sacks. People shoveled snow and warmed hands over little coal fires. Newspapers were stacked on the street corner. She caught the headline: **GUSTAFSON REVEALS A DISASTER**. Carriages jostled by. Street workers swept. Vendors closed their trolleys and gathered around a fire as a blacksmith hammered at a horseshoe. Jessica emerged into the town square. It hadn't changed from when she was last there as a young woman. Like her father said in his letter, she hoped they could make it work again, too.

She took a breath and entered the shop.

After looking everywhere, Jeronicus was in the very last place she had thought to check.

"Daddy." Jessica stepped foot into his workshop.

He froze, then turned from his worktable and looked at her standing in the doorway. They regarded one another, after so long. "Jessica," he breathed in awe.

Jessica was shocked to find him there, of all places—and with a full scraggly beard! Thirty years had added a bit of weight, and a hunch, yet he seemed the exact same to her. She clasped her hands diplomatically. "I thought I'd come get Journey early. I hope she hasn't been too much of a bother. It was nice of you to even want to spend time with her at all."

"Actually, I never . . ." He took a breath, stopping himself from correcting her—that he'd not actually been the one to send the letter. "Never could have imagined she'd be such a delight." A warm, familiar smile washed over his face. "And— And she's quite the inventor!" he added with pride.

"She must've gotten that from you." Jessica averted her eyes.

He pointed wanly at her. "Or you."

Despite his decency, she kept her guard up. "We should leave now if we're to make it by morning." She turned through the doorway.

"Jessica, I'm sorry." He reached his arms out toward her. He'd realized that she'd reminded him of the loss of his wife, so he had unwittingly pushed her away, and for that, he was truly sorry. No one deserved that kind of neglect—especially not a child, and one so very special.

She slowly faced him. "For what?" She advanced across the protesting floorboards. "For giving up? For making me feel like it was my fault that things turned out the way they did?" Her expression exposed all the pain and suffering she'd been secretly carrying. "Do you know how many times I went to my mailbox, hoping for . . . *something* to let me know you still cared? That— That you even thought about me at all?" Her eyes misted with devastated tears.

"I thought about you every day," he confessed softly.

"Every day." He crossed to a cabinet, wrenched open the door, and stepped aside as an avalanche of envelopes poured out and formed a colorful pile at his feet.

She eyed them, but did not move.

He reached down and scooped up a handful. "Given everything that happened, I wasn't sure that you wanted to hear from me, so I didn't send these letters," he confessed.

She hesitantly took one and opened it with trembling fingers. "'Dear Jessica, I wish I could make up for all my faults as a parent. I wanted you to have the world,'" she read aloud. "'Reach into the heavens, pull down the stars, just so they could shine on you.'" She choked up, but kept reading. "'Not just read about a happily ever after; I wanted to be the one to give it to you. Jeronicus Jangle, the greatest inventor of all, who only wishes he were . . .'" Her eyes welled with gladness. She looked up at him.

"'The greatest father of all,'" Jeronicus finished gently.

She blinked back the tears and returned her gaze to the letter.

"Journey reminds me so much of you and your mother," Jeronicus shared. "I want to be there for her like I should have been there for you."

She regarded him, and was moved. He had done the impossible. He had changed.

He tilted her chin up and grinned. "Seeing you has made me smile."

She gave a small smile in turn.

"I'm sorry. I love you so much," he professed.

"I love you too, Daddy," she revealed.

They embraced. They had made it work again. There was hope.

Jessica let her tears fall, and Jeronicus let his sleeve soak them up.

Finally, they parted.

Jeronicus handed his kerchief to her. "I'm gonna go wake up Journey, if you don't mind. Say our so-longs and goodbyes." He walked to the door.

"If she's asleep, we could stay, and maybe take a morning bus," Jessica offered.

His eyebrows rose in bemusement.

"Maybe we could spend Christmas here?" she said. "If it's all right with you." It would be Christmas in a few short hours, and she was no longer in a rush to return to Nesbitt Cottage.

He beamed. "That would be very all right with me."

She nodded as another happy tear rolled down her cheek, and she blotted it with his kerchief. Her eyes settled on the Buddy 3000 lying on the worktable, and she let out a little laugh. "Is that . . . ?" She walked toward the robot, amazed her father had actually made an invention she'd dreamed up as a girl. She never fathomed there'd come a day she'd meet Buddy.

"The Buddy 3000," Jeronicus said. "Or what's left of him."

"You did it!" she said.

He joined her side. "I was hoping to put it back together for Journey. She's taken quite a liking to him."

"If we start now, maybe . . ." Jessica computed the timeline in her head. "Maybe we could put it together by morning." She gazed up at her father from the robot's broken heart.

Jeronicus nodded. It was more than he could ever have wished for—inventing again with his daughter by his side. He eyed his workstation, not sure where to begin.

Jessica lifted tiny cogs off the table and lightly pressed them into his palm.

He stared at her. He'd missed that. She was who had been missing all these years.

Jessica regarded her leather-bound book of inventions lying open beside the robot, grazing her fingers across the eccentric designs with nostalgia. Then she examined the robot.

"Symmetry brings synchronicity," Jeronicus said.

"Which is the stability of it all," Jessica added.

"You've been reading my notes," he remarked.

"I think you've been reading *my* notes," she corrected genially.

They laughed, and began to work on fixing and mending all that had been broken.

Gradually, Christmas-morning sun streamed into the workshop, along with the festive sounds of the square full of jolly people below as Jeronicus and Jessica put the finishing touches on Buddy, who stood on the table, gleaming as if he were brand new. The emergency surgery had worked!

Jessica used a tool to blow pressurized air into the glass cube, then aimed the nozzle at her father and let out a tiny spurt of air at his face. She chuckled. They'd had fun not sleeping a wink, but it'd made them both a bit loopy.

Journey charged into the workshop in her nightgown. "Grandpa J, I—" She stopped in her tracks when she saw her mother seated beside him. "Mommy!" And there was Buddy, better than ever. "Grandpa J, you did it!" she cheered. She raced over and wrapped him a warm hug.

"Had a little help," he admitted.

"Mommy!" Journey hugged Jessica, inhaling her chamomile scent. She'd missed that.

"Hello, baby," Jessica replied.

"Had a *lot* of help," Jeronicus amended. "From both of you." He grinned.

Journey admired Buddy with eager eyes. "Now all you have to do is press the on button."

Jeronicus regarded the robot with uncertainty. Jessica rested a solacing hand on him, and he took a deep breath and stood, Journey watching as he slotted the cube into Buddy.

Jeronicus closed his eyes. "I believe. Just believe."

Pinpricks of light sparkled in Buddy's otherwise dark eyes.

Journey beamed up at her grandfather. He was doing it!

The gears began to turn.

Buddy's eyes widened at him.

Jeronicus raised his eyebrows. "Buddy?"

He was no longer dormant, but adoring, and very much awake.

"You're alive," Jeronicus breathed, exchanging a cheery smile with Journey. "Glad to see you, Buddy," he told the robot. "Glad you're here." After so long, the Jangles were all together.

Even Joanne, whose presence he felt stronger than ever.

Just then, a voice rang out from the ground floor.

"Jeronicus Jangle! Present yourself immediately!"

The Jangles weren't about to be
duped by Gustafson. Not again.
And especially not on Christmas.

Chapter Twenty-Four

"Gustafson." Downstairs, Journey had found him standing at Jeronicus's desk.

He spun around and removed his top hat. "Well hello, young lady."

Jeronicus and Jessica emerged on the landing. "What is the meaning of this?" he asked.

Two constables moved to detain him.

"The robot that you stole from me," Gustafson accused coldly.

"To the dungeon with him!" Don Juan said from where he stood on the desk. "Yes. You."

"I demand that you arrest him at once, right now!" Gustafson ordered the constables, who struggled to keep their holds on Jeronicus's wriggling wrists.

"For what?" Jessica demanded. She would not allow her father to be wrongfully policed.

Journey advanced on him. "You're the *real* thief."

"A *thief* couldn't have these." Gustafson slipped a page out from his cloak. He unfolded it and showed the sketches to the constables. "The designs for the robot that *I* slaved over."

"Restless days and sleepless nights," Don Juan piped in, for effect.

"I wanted to give up so many times, but I didn't. I—"

"We," Don Juan corrected him.

"Persevered," Gustafson continued. "Knowing that one day, I—"

"We," Don Juan corrected again.

Gustafson shot daggers at him. "Would realize my dream." His voice had a put-on sadness to it, and he pulled the large page taut, showcasing it. "Proof! In black and white."

Journey snatched it. "And blue!"

"¿Azul?" Don Juan inquired.

She crossed to the lamp and flicked it on. As she held the designs under the bulb, radiant blue words began to materialize across the page in a scrolling, looping handwriting, like ribbons.

Property of Jeronicus Jangle

One of the constables read it aloud.

Journey held the page up high.

The other constable regarded it and looked to Gustafson. "Explain this at once!"

Gustafson stammered. "It's— It's . . ."

"I can explain." Journey boldly approached him. "After I ran into Mr. Gustafson, I was afraid he would try to steal the Buddy 3000."

Gustafson held his pointer finger up to his mouth in an effort to silence her.

"So," she continued, "I marked the design. For proof."

The constables freed Jeronicus, who looked proudly at his brilliant Journey.

Gustafson's face hardened. He'd been found out at long last. "Uh-oh. Just arrest Mr. Jangle!"

"You told me those were *your* inventions!" Don Juan accused, lying. "Did you lie? Are you a thief? Yes. You." Don Juan then ran across the desk. "Jeronicus, save me!" he cried.

"I'll take the matador," Jeronicus said. "It's my invention, after all."

"I am home! Mi rey," Don Juan said with relief. "I've missed you!" he said to Jeronicus with feigned affection. "I like your hair. Did you do that yourself?"

Jeronicus lifted him. "Finally, children everywhere will be able to love you."

"I am extremely lovable," he said arrogantly from Jeronicus's hand. "Puppy dog eyes! Baby kitten eyes!"

"After I reprogram you," Jeronicus concluded.

"Reprogram? Reprogram what?! I am and forever will be one and only one of a k—!"

Jeronicus opened a panel in Don Juan's back and disconnected him, then set him down on the desk and stared at Gustafson as the constables stomped over to him.

"What are you doing?" Gustafson asked them.

The constables roughly grabbed him.

"This doesn't make any sense!" Gustafson argued, wrestling against them. "You're taking the word of a ten-year-old child! I am a respected member of the community! Are you kidding? I mean, look at that child! Look at that girl! There's evil in her eyes!"

The constables steered him down the mahogany staircase and toward the front doors.

"Wait, wait, wait," Jeronicus said, chasing after them. "I have something for him." He walked to a desk by the entranceway and pulled out the decrepit bottom drawer.

The constables halted in the doorway, holding Gustafson still, and everyone watched Jeronicus, who produced a rectangular box wrapped in paper and tied with a length of green silk ribbon.

"I had it to give it to you that night." He approached Gustafson. "But then you were gone." He handed the present to Gustafson, a gift thirty years in the making.

Gustafson untied the ribbon and opened the gift. It was a simple wooden box. He flipped the lid to find a small metal contraption nestled inside. He teared up. "A gyroscopic stabilizer."

Jeronicus looked kindly back at him. "For your Twirling Whirly."

Gustafson gritted his teeth to hold back his tears. Jeronicus was as generous as he had always been, while Gustafson's heart had only grown colder. He had waited all his youth for a token of Jeronicus's time, and when he finally got it, he felt unworthy of such a gracious gesture.

"I would have shown you everything, if only you'd waited," Jeronicus added.

As Gustafson looked up at Jeronicus, he felt like a child again. He had waited for no tomorrows, but tomorrow had been worth waiting for, in the end. Now it was too late. Eyes misting with tears, he grappled with what to say, but "thank you" hadn't quite been introduced to his vocabulary yet.

The constables guided him from the shop and into the police carriage on the street.

Gustafson glanced back at Jeronicus one last time.

The inventor, old and grayed, cast his eyes down.

"Oh dear, oh dear, oh dear," came a voice, and Jeronicus looked up to see Mr. Delacroix strolling toward him through the shop's front doors, walking with a harried gait.

"Mr. Delacroix," Jeronicus greeted him.

"Merry Christmas, old friend." Mr. Delacroix shook his hand, then removed his hat and tipped it at Jessica and Journey. "Ladies." He came face-to-face with Jeronicus, and his good cheer soured. "I'm sorry it's come to this, but—"

A trilling from the upper-level landing siphoned his attention away.

There was Buddy, levitating over the bannister and gliding down toward them.

Mr. Delacroix cowered behind Jeronicus. "What in heaven's . . . ?" Then he stepped out and rested a hand on Jeronicus's shoulder as the robot hovered serenely over the cash register.

"It's something sensational," Jeronicus said proudly.

Mr. Delacroix moved toward the robot. "Yes, it's—"

"Something spectacular." Jeronicus followed on his heels.

"More than that, it's—"

"Something *revolutionary*," they said in unison.

Jeronicus gestured. "It's the Buddy 3000!"

"The Bud— The *what*?" Mr. Delacroix asked, perplexed.

"It's a robot," Jessica asserted.

Flabbergasted, he wheeled on them, brows furrowed. "I beg your pardon?"

"A flying robot!" Journey added with a merry nod.

His eyes bugged. "Is such a thing possible?" he asked Jeronicus.

"Something sensational!" Buddy said from the air. *"Something spectacular! Something revolutionary!"*

"It *talks*?" inquired an astounded Mr. Delacroix.

Jeronicus gave a self-assured nod. "It talks."

The banker turned to Journey and Jessica. "It talks," he

said, to which they nodded smugly. He faced the robot. "You *talk*!" Mr. Delacroix's eyes sparkled. "By Jove, Jeronicus, you've done it! You are a genius, my old friend."

Jeronicus meant to state that it had been a team effort, but Mr. Delacroix cut him off with a finger wag. "No, no, no, no, no! If I know anything, there's more where that came from."

"I have thirty years' worth of notes," Jeronicus replied. And now that he believed in the impossible again, thereby reviving his magic, the possibilities of bringing all of those divine designs to life were limitless.

"I have no doubt! Oh, look at you! I could kiss you!" He smooched Jeronicus on the cheek then firmly shook his hand. "From now on, whatever you need, the bank will give you for the rest of your life!" It was all Jeronicus could have dreamed of.

Buddy landed softly on the countertop.

Mr. Delacroix rushed out the door, shouting, "He's a genius! It's spectacular!" He waved his hat back at them. "It's a merry, merry Christmas indeed!"

And so it was—even for Gustafson, who, despite being carted off in the police carriage as it jostled off down Chancer Street, had learned the error of his ways—and discovered his heart.

As for Jeronicus, even when life had knocked him down, he'd figured out how to get back up.

With a little help.

With a *lot* of help.

The Jangles may have been lost,

but they finally found their way.

All their lives they'd waited for this day.

Chapter Twenty-Five

With a buzzing chime and a cheerful *whoosh*, Buddy took to the air again.

Slowly, Jeronicus began to rise off the ground, too. "Whoa, whoa, whoa! What's going on? Buddy? Put me down. Put me down." He floated up higher and higher.

"Grandpa J, just let go!" Journey encouraged him.

He was high above them now, with Buddy circling him. He let out a nervous little laugh. "Whoa! I'm actually flying!" He got the hang of it, swimming through the air.

"Wow, Grandpa J!" Journey hooted.

"You're doing great, Daddy," Jessica praised.

From outside, townspeople celebrating Christmas pressed their happy faces to the frosted windowpanes, gasping as they took in the marvelous feat taking place inside. Chuckling children raced in from the square. Other people stepped foot into the shop, enchanted. What was this? Jaws dropped. Eyes shone wide. People oohed and aahed, watching the robot and old man dancing in the air.

"Hey, everyone!" Jeronicus called down to the crowd gathering in the doorway. He held his arms out wide. "Jangles and Things is open for business!" he announced. His pawnshop had served to give life to an object that had lost it, a cherished possession restored to its former glory. Who knew that the object he'd end up resurrecting and reviving would be his own ticking heart?

All had been restored.

"A World of Wishes and Wonder!" he added happily.

Everyone cheered and applauded. It was a merry, merry Christmas indeed!

Ms. Johnston squeezed through the throng in a red-and-green-striped dress and hat. "Jerry! You get down from there this instant!" No matter how much she longed to become a *Mrs.* again, she'd be there for Jeronicus no matter what he chose to pursue deep down in his heart.

Everyone laughed and whooped.

Just then, Edison fearlessly ran into the shop with a huge grin, and rose up in the air to meet Jeronicus and Buddy, elated. Journey and Jessica levitated up after him, laughing joyfully.

And so, Gustafson's Factory was taken over by Jeronicus, its garish *G* replaced with a jazzy *J*. And everything that was stolen from Jeronicus was returned to him. New inventions joined the ranks of old ones, like Journey's cuckoo clock, whose wooden songbird could also fly!

Journey also wrote a book about her eccentric, wonderful family, one that was not for sale—and one that was truly one of a kind. A tale for the Jangles to pass on for generations to come, to be told during story time, during just the right moment when one needed it most . . .

THE INVENTION OF JERONICUS JANGLE.

And they laughed and sang and danced,

just like flames in a crackling hearth.

If you look close enough,

you can see the magic, too.

So long as you believe.

NESBITT COTTAGE

53 Lenox Road, Summit

December 18th, 1890

Dear Father,

I've decided to let Journey stay with you until Christmas. She's an inquisitive girl, but well mannered. Like you said, it's time you both got to know each other. I'll be there to pick her up on Christmas morning. I hope you are well.

Love,

Jessica

Acknowledgments

Heartfelt thanks to Scott Stuber, Nick Nesbitt, and the entire Netflix team for your belief in this project. To our *Jingle Jangle* family, thank you for the love and passion you shared in bringing this story to life. We did it!! See ya in the sequel!

To Albert Lee, thank you for making this experience fun and for introducing us to our new publishing family. To Casey McIntyre, Jess Harriton, and all of Razorbill and Penguin Random House, thank you for helping to put the magic on the page. You made it possible to make this journey a wonderfully magical ride in another form.

A special thank you to Eric Geron for your phenomenal vision, wonder, and excitement. We couldn't have done it without you.